HOME, SWEET IRISH HOME

MICHELE BROUDER

Editing by Jessica Peirce

Book Cover Design by www.madcatdesigns.net

Home, Sweet Irish Home

To God be the Glory.

CHAPTER ONE

"Do you believe in love at first sight?" April asked. She wore a wistful expression as she stared out the front window of Maggie Moran's health food shop, Slainte Mhaith.

Maggie didn't have to think about it. "Absolutely not."

Her shop assistant took a sip of her nettle tea and continued to stare out the window. Maggie loved April like a younger sister, but sometimes she wished she did more working and less staring.

April set her fine bone china teacup down on the counter next to the cash register. She folded her arms across her crocheted granny-square vest. "Can you imagine what that would feel like? To see someone across a room and your eyes meet and something clicks?"

Looking at the younger woman with her waif-like face and fine blonde hair, Maggie realized there'd be no work out of April if Maggie didn't finish this conversation to her assistant's satisfaction.

"Soul mates?" April pressed.

Maggie shook her head. She was what some people would call too practical. Too sensible. But it was who she was, and she wasn't going to change.

"Destiny? Fate?" April asked. She waved her hand around the small interior of the shop. "It's funny that you're so black-and-white about things. You'd think with the shop and the salt lamps and the herbs and the homemade soap that you'd have more of a New Age attitude."

Maggie frowned at her assistant. "My attitude is one of good health and getting as close to nature as you can to achieve it." She was thoughtful for a moment. "Isn't it even in the shop's name? *Slainte mhaith*: good health."

April was not impressed. "What about romance?"

"What about it?" Maggie asked. When Maggie heard the word "romance," intimate candlelit moments and grand gestures came to mind. Ideas she liked, although they always seemed to be happening for someone else.

"Don't you have any romance in your soul?" April asked.

"What does that even mean?" Maggie asked. She pressed her lips together into a thin line. A part of her bristled at the question. It insinuated that she was somehow lacking. She did not want to have this discussion. There were some things that were private.

"Don't you want to fall in love someday?"

Maggie would not divulge her hopes and dreams to April or to anyone else. "If it happens, it happens, if it doesn't, it doesn't." She was pretty content with her life as it was.

April frowned, blowing on the surface of her tea to cool it down. "That sounds kind of bleak."

Maggie shrugged, not too concerned with how it sounded. "There can be beauty in bleakness."

"I'll light a candle for you," April said.

"Unnecessary," Maggie said with a sigh. April liked to light candles. It was her thing. "I think it's best to get to know someone over time, develop a friendship first and have that as a basis for a relationship," Maggie said. She would have preferred it this way. Love at first sight? *No thanks!*

April grimaced. "That doesn't sound very exciting."

"No, but isn't it nice?" Maggie asked. She wondered what the problem was. Wasn't there comfort in the long-term commitment?

"What about passion or sparks?" April asked.

"Trust me, you can get burned with some sparks," Maggie observed. Then again, what business had she giving relationship advice? None, she decided. Just over thirty, she could count on one hand the number of dates she'd been on in the last two years. For one reason or another, it just never seemed to work out. More than once, she'd been left disappointed. She made a pointed gesture of looking at the clock above the door. "We'd better get back to work." Working with April or better yet, getting April to do some actual work, was a lot like herding cats. It needed constant attention.

Though she wasn't about to admit it to April, Maggie was hopeful she would fall in love again someday. For real. With someone who loved her just as she was. A long time ago, she'd realized she was too different from the mainstream to attract more than a passing interest from most men. Too nerdy. Too quirky. She'd accepted that about herself. The practical side of her thought it wouldn't be the end of the world if it didn't happen. She had her shop and the dogs and the cat and was content.

It was time to throw a bucket of cold water on April's daydreaming.

Maggie looked around the shop. "We need to get the stock unloaded before I go. Did you call Nora over at Mother Nature about the part of the shipment being missing?"

April blinked. "I'll do that right now."

There was no more talk of falling in love at first sight, and Maggie was relieved. The rest of the afternoon flew, and between the two of them they got all the shelves restocked.

Just before closing, a teenaged boy opened the door and crossed the threshold, looking around. As April was busy with Mrs. Maroney with queries about what the older woman could use for her stiff knee, Maggie stepped out from behind the counter. The boy looked to be about seventeen, with T-zone acne and sun-streaked brown hair. His complexion was caramel, as if he were someone used to spending their life outdoors, or at least who lived in a sunny clime. He hesitated near the doorway as his eyes darted around the place. He bit his lip.

"Can I help you?" Maggie asked with a smile.

"Um, yeah," he said. "I was looking for some vegan snacks."

An American accent. Maggie was surprised. They usually didn't get too many Americans in Ballygap. She gave him a reassuring smile. "Then you've come to the right place. Follow me."

She took a small wicker basket from the colorful stack in front of the counter and headed into the interior of the shop, indicating that he should follow her. She pointed out various snacks as they went. "There's some wasabi-coated almonds, and there's some vegan chocolate. And my favorite, chocolate-covered coconut bars."

He nodded but said nothing.

"Were you looking for sweet or savory?"

The boy looked up and gave her a shy smile. "Both."

It was Maggie's turn to nod. "How long have you been a vegan?"

"Almost a year."

"I commend your commitment," she said.

The boy blushed and looked down. "Thanks."

He must be holidaying somewhere nearby with his family, Maggie thought. Their small seaside town was built up around a horseshoe-shaped inlet in County Clare in the west of Ireland, and in a month or so, during the height of summer, it would be packed with tourists, albeit very few from abroad. There was nothing else there but the beach, and it was just a little too off the beaten track.

As she showed him various snacks, he'd pick something up, study it, and then toss it and a couple more into the basket.

"How long are you in Ballygap for?"

"The summer," he answered. "My dad's here on business."

"Very good," she said. "My name's Maggie, if you ever have any questions. Stop in any time."

He nodded and mumbled thanks. He lifted his head and spotted the menu board behind the counter.

"Oh great, you have coffee and tea."

"Would you like one?" Maggie asked.

He studied the board and decided. "Can I have a matcha with oat milk?"

As she made his beverage, Maggie wondered about him. Were American boys anything like Irish boys? She was no expert, but most seemed to be sports mad, interested in any activity that involved a ball being thrown, chased, caught, or kicked around. This boy seemed different, and life would be difficult for a teenager who wasn't interested in the same things as his peers. It might only be Maggie's opinion, but she'd based it on personal experience and keen observation.

———— *ele* ————

Once the clock struck five, April grabbed her quilted satchel and bid Maggie goodbye. Maggie took her time, lingering in her shop. She loved being there after the doors were locked, when all was quiet.

Half an hour later, she exited through the front door, locking everything up and setting the alarm. Her bike leaned against the side wall of the shop. She donned her backpack, put on her helmet, and pulled the bike away from the shop wall. She swung her leg over, got comfortable on the seat, and began pedaling. At most, it was a ten-minute bike ride to her house. She stayed on the narrow road, close to the footpath, following it toward the bluffs and the sea.

The town was built on a series of natural hills and dips. And though the town center was mostly located in a dip, her health food shop stood at the top of a small hill at the fork of the main road, which then split off into two roads, each leading out of town and away from the ocean. The left fork led to the caravan park, and the right led you to farmland and away from Ballygap.

As she cycled toward home, she noticed a man in running gear up ahead on the footpath, pounding the pavement. She raised an eyebrow in appreciation of his well-muscled thighs and calves. She hadn't seen him before; he must be a tourist.

Her home soon came into view: a cottage with a thatched roof that had been in her family for hundreds of years. Her ancestors had been fishermen. The cottage stood at the edge of the bluff against the backdrop of the Atlantic. She never tired of the sight of it, although it needed a fresh coat of paint. The apricot color had long since faded. It had been her home for the last fifteen years, since she'd arrived to live with her grandparents.

The cries of gulls increased in volume the nearer she got to the water.

She parked her bike against the front of the cottage and dug around her bag for her keys. After she unlocked the fire-engine-red Dutch door, her two dogs came bounding toward her. She bent down and gave each one an affectionate pat and a rub on the head.

Maggie looked around her home, wondering where the cat was. As if on cue, there was the sound of a crash in the bedroom. Maggie rolled her eyes. Twinkle, the cat, was notorious for knocking things over. He loved cruising along the tight spaces of dresser surfaces, tabletops, and countertops, among the knick-knacks and other things. She'd given up years ago trying to break him of the habit.

She glanced at Rufus, a black Labrador retriever and the younger of the two dogs. She nodded toward him and said, "Get the cat, will you?"

Within minutes, Rufus returned, carrying the ginger cat by the scruff of his neck.

"Good boy," Maggie said, patting the dog's head affectionately. The dog responded with an enthusiastic wag of his tail.

She stood at the door and called for her entourage. "Come on, let's go." Rufus continued to carry Twinkle, and Daisy, the Irish setter, trotted out the door.

Maggie lifted a white straw trilby hat off the peg by the door. It had been Granddad's. Aunt Eileen had bought it for him when she'd been in Florida, and Granddad had taken an immediate shine to it, trading his traditional plaid flat cap for it. After he died, Maggie had taken to wearing it to protect her face from the sun. She picked up a basket she kept near the door and looped it over her arm.

Before she closed the cottage door behind her, she smiled at the interior. Not much had changed from the time when her grandparents had been alive. Nana had only been gone a few years, but Granddad had been gone for almost a decade. The dark yellow walls remained, as did the St. Brigid's cross made from rushes above the presses in the kitchen and her grandfather's bodhran, hanging on the wall to the right of the fireplace. Her grandmother's rocker flanked the left side of the hearth. Sometimes, she could still see her grandmother sitting there, and the slow, gentle motion of the rocking as her knitting needles flew. But Maggie had added her own touches: candles littered the place, and there was the new sofa and the recent addition of a flat-screen television. She'd also purchased some original artwork from Irish artists that now adorned the walls.

Maggie skipped the narrow footpath that would join with the main path that ran parallel along the cliffs. Instead, she went behind her cottage and headed down the well-worn path leading to the beach below. Being near the water or just wading through the surf always recalibrated her.

Maggie pulled her knit shawl closer around her shoulders as she navigated her way down to the beach. As soon as they reached it, Rufus dumped the cat and ran back and forth along the sand. Daisy walked alongside Maggie, not straying far. Although the sun shone, there was a bitter wind blowing in off the Atlantic. Her hat blew off, and Maggie's long black hair whipped around her face. She chased the tumbling hat down the beach, and when she caught it, she wedged the brim tightly under the basket handle. The ocean was a stormy shade of gray, and waves crested, and seafoam crashed upon the small beach. She closed her eyes, breathing in the salty air, the smell of brine strong. The horizon was blurry and gray. Rain coming in. She'd better hurry and collect her seaweed before they all got soaked. The remains of a rotted currach, a boat once used by her great-great-grandfather for fishing, leaned against the large stone boulders that shored up the bottom of the cliff.

For the next half hour, she walked along the shore gathering seaweed, or kelp as some called it, and putting it in the woven basket she carried on her arm. Once her basket was full, she headed to the rocky incline that would take her off the beach. Rufus ran ahead on the sandy path, disappearing over the crest of the hill, and Maggie called out after him.

She pressed her lips together. "Oh, Rufus." At two, he still had a lot of puppy in him.

She was halfway up the path when she heard Rufus bark in the distance. There was no letup and Maggie picked up her pace, feeling the muscles in her calves and thighs tighten as she hurried up the steep incline. It sounded like his playful bark, which meant he'd met someone on the path. Rufus loved people, but not all people loved Rufus or dogs in general.

"Come on," Maggie said to Daisy, who was trailing behind her. She glanced around for the cat but didn't see him. Twinkle would eventually make his way back home. Eager to catch up with the mutinous dog, Maggie broke into a trot. Once she cleared the hill, she pulled up short, catching her breath.

"Oh no," she muttered. Rufus now had the attention of the jogger she'd seen earlier.

"Rufus!" she called. The dog had found someone to pet him. That was Rufus's problem. He thought it was people's job to shower him with affection.

Rufus now sat next to the man, who was bent over him, rubbing his head and scratching behind his ears and talking to him. Maggie's eyes widened in alarm at how near they were to the cliff's edge. Afraid of heights herself, Maggie never went near it. Fifty yards away sat a stark reminder: a simple wooden crucifix with the name of a young man who'd fallen to his death five years previous.

When she approached them, the man straightened up. He blinked and his mouth opened slightly before he composed himself, putting his hands on his hips and flashing a smile that revealed perfect white teeth. Although older than her—somewhere in his mid-forties, she'd guess—he was handsome. His face was rugged: tanned and weathered, with fine lines at the corners of his eyes and traversing his forehead. His golden hair, broad cheekbones, and tanned skin the color of caramel suggested a life spent outdoors. The wind whipped through his hair.

"This your dog?" he asked. The accent was American.

Rufus nudged the man's hand, wanting to be petted. The man laughed and obliged.

Maggie nodded, forgetting to speak as she drank him in. What was it about him that made her stop, blink, and stare? The sunny looks? That sculpted face? The confidence? His easygoing manner? She couldn't remember the last time she'd been tongue-tied around a man. It was as rare an occurrence as an appearance of the Christmas star.

"He's a great-looking dog," the man remarked.

That was true. Rufus's coat was like black silk, and he had the broad shoulders and face typical of Labrador retrievers. It was his size many people found intimidating when they met him. He'd been the alpha male of the litter and was bigger than most Labs, with longer than average legs.

The man shifted on his feet. His running shorts ended just above the knee, revealing muscular, tanned legs.

Maggie tried not to stare. Or whimper.

Rufus ran around the man, perilously close to the edge.

"Look, would you mind stepping away from the edge?" Maggie blurted.

The man grinned. "Are you afraid I'll fall?"

"Yes, as a matter of fact I am," she said with a nod to the nearby memorial.

The American glanced over at it and stepped away from the edge, closer to the footpath where Maggie stood. It relieved her that Rufus followed him.

"The ground is unstable at the edge of the cliff," she explained. "People stand too close to the edge, not knowing that it might only be an overhang with nothing of substance beneath it."

He took another step back. "Thanks. I had no idea," he said.

The man reached down and petted the dog again. Rufus was in his glory. The man glanced over at Daisy, who had remained standing behind Maggie. Daisy wasn't as impressed with the stranger as Rufus had been. With a nod to the setter, the man asked, "Is she afraid of people?"

"She takes time to warm up." Maggie didn't bother going into Daisy's backstory. Daisy was a rescue dog who, in the first year of her life, had suffered abuse at the hands of her male owner. As a result, Daisy feared all men. But with a lot of patience and determination on Maggie's part, there'd been improvement. Daisy would never be as gregarious as Rufus, but she let people she knew pet her. After a while.

"Jake Ballard," the stranger said, extending his hand in greeting. Maggie shook it, liking the way his warm hand dwarfed hers.

"Maggie. Maggie Moran," she said. "Are you here on holidays?"

"Actually, I'm here on business, so it will be a working vacation," he replied. His reply was like that of the teenage boy earlier in her shop and Maggie narrowed her eyes, thinking she saw a resemblance and wondering if they were father and son. Curious, she wanted to ask what kind of business he did, but she refrained, not wanting to appear nosy.

"Do you live here?" he asked.

"Yes, I run the health food shop in town," she volunteered.

"Health food," he repeated, his eyes not leaving her face. "I'll have to check it out someday."

Maggie felt her cheeks tinge pink at the prospect of seeing him again. There was a part of her that hoped he would follow through on that.

A sudden gust of wind lifted the hat out of her hand, and it sailed away from her again.

"Oh no!" she said, reaching for it but missing.

Jake ran after it, but the breeze lifted it higher and higher until it sailed right over the cliff. Maggie joined Jake near the edge—but not too near—and looked over. Granddad's hat landed on a wave and headed out to sea.

"My hat . . ."

"I'm sorry about that," Jake said.

She offered him a smile tinged with sadness. "It's not your fault. But thanks for trying to catch it."

He nodded. "I'd better get on my way." He rubbed the back of his head and looked around, hesitating. "I don't want to keep you."

Maggie wanted to tell him he wasn't keeping her from anything, but her voice died in her throat.

"I look forward to seeing you again, Maggie Moran," he said with a smile. And he jogged off. He hadn't gone far when he looked back one final time and waved.

Rufus leaped after the man, but Maggie grabbed his collar. "Oh no you don't."

Maggie, Rufus, and Daisy stood on the footpath watching the fine form of Jake Ballard getting smaller and smaller the farther he got away from them. Finally, Maggie turned around and headed toward her home, replaying the interaction with Jake in her mind. By the time she reached her cottage, she was smiling, the lost hat forgotten.

CHAPTER TWO

J AKE RESUMED HIS RUN and headed away from the woman
and her dogs. It required a Herculean effort on his part not
to stay and remain in Maggie Moran's presence. She was as
beautiful as the Irish landscape.

Summer in Ireland didn't mean the weather was hot. Jake
wondered if they ever had a scorcher of a day here like they
were inclined to have back home in California. This was his
second trip to Ireland, and a few things stood out to him. First,
the hospitality of the Irish people. Everywhere he went, people
talked to him. They were open and friendly. He found himself
impressed with the sky. At night, there was a swath of stars
across the canvas of the night sky, too many to count. Probably
had something to do with the lack of pollution. The scenery
was beautiful. Everywhere you turned, there was something to
look at. It was never ending between the cliffs, the ocean, the
sand dunes, and the hilly green pastures. Of all the places he'd
been in the world, this one was shaping up to be one of his
favorites.

Since his arrival, Jake had run every morning, a habit he'd developed years ago. But because of an early meeting with a local councilman that day, he'd had to forgo his daily run until the afternoon. When he'd heard Maggie's Irish accent carrying in on the breeze as she called for her dog, he'd been intrigued, and waited to see who belonged to that lyrical voice. When she appeared from the beach down below, he'd drawn in an involuntary breath, thinking he was seeing a spectral image. Her long, dark, curly hair blew around her from the wind shifting in off the ocean. It was inky black, like a moonless sky at midnight. And her skin was so pale it appeared translucent. But her eyes, big and blue like sapphires and fringed with velvet lashes, stood out a mile away. His first thought was, where had she been hiding all his life?

He pounded the pavement harder and picked up his speed, as if by doing so he could push any thoughts of the Irishwoman from his mind. He reminded himself that his purpose in Ireland was business. And no matter how attracted he was to her, he'd only be there for a few months before heading on to the next project, hopefully in a sunnier and warmer clime.

Jake's other concern was his seventeen-year-old son, Noah. He'd brought him along on the trip thinking it would do them good, or that's what he told himself. Noah was a good kid, but he was having difficulty in high school fitting in, and Jake worried about him. He hoped he'd be able to toughen the boy up over the next three months. If nothing else, it was a perfect opportunity to get his son off his current vegan phase.

A glance at his Fitbit and he knew he had to get back to the house soon if he wanted to shower before his scheduled call with his father. As he jogged away from the ocean and the cliffs, he ran along the footpaths until he came to the town center.

He passed shops, a grocery store, a church, and a medical center.

Their rental house was located just as the shops petered out and residential homes appeared. The three-bedroom bungalow with its stone facade was tucked between two others like it, stretching long behind a stone wall. The walls were painted a tan color, reminding him of waffles. The owner was away in Australia for twelve months, and though not ideal, the place was suitable. Jake had rented separate office space in town next to a dress shop, and that's where he had set up his business.

He lingered in the asphalt driveway, doing some cool-down exercises.

The front door to the bungalow opened and Noah appeared, gangly and disheveled, holding a water bottle.

"Could you not do that out in the open?" Noah asked.

"Do what?" Jake asked.

"Those exercises. Come in, Dad, before anyone sees you. You look like a lunatic out there."

"It's important to cool down," Jake explained.

Noah grumbled something unintelligible and disappeared into the house, leaving the door open for Jake.

On his previous visit, Jake had been disappointed that there was no five-star or even a four-star hotel in Ballygap. But as it turned out, the bungalow better suited him and Noah. Once the resort was built, there'd be a five-star hotel where he'd be able to stay any time he returned. If he ever returned.

_____ℓℓℓ_____

The following evening after work, he took the footpath out of town to walk along the cliffs. As he walked, he took everything in: the Atlantic to the west, and the wild grass and the bright flowers that grew amongst it: gorse, fuchsia, and montbretia.

He passed a small cottage at the cliff's edge on his left but kept walking, his eyes on the tract of farmland to his right that went on for as far as the eye could see. The McDougal farm was a vast property whose owner had died years ago, and now the fields were overgrown. But the site had a lot of potential for a golf course and resort, as he'd concluded when he visited Ballygap the previous winter, making day trips from his hotel in Limerick city to scout the seaside town for potential development. He'd had two other places in mind, as well, in Jamaica and Germany, but ultimately, he'd decided that Ireland was the place to build.

The sun was beginning its western descent, and the landscape was filtered through pastel colors. He liked this walk, and he liked the thought of owning the McDougal farm. There were a couple of adjoining properties that would have to be purchased, but he was getting ahead of himself. First, they had to secure the purchase, and that was based on planning permission.

As he walked along, he nodded to a few walkers that passed him on the footpath. He had to admit to some disappointment in not running into Maggie. He wondered where she lived. It couldn't be too far from where they'd met, as she'd had her pets with her.

He walked as far as he could, past the farm itself and toward the neighboring homes on the other side of it. Then he turned around and headed home.

When he arrived at their rental, Noah was puttering around the kitchen, gathering ingredients and piling them on the island. On top, a vegan cookbook was open to a recipe. There were bowls, measuring devices, and utensils laid out on the island.

"I thought we'd go out for dinner," Jake said.

Without looking up, Noah replied, "Nah, I'm good."

"What are you making?" Jake asked.

"It's called a Buddha bowl," Noah answered. He bent over, studying the cookbook, his look intense.

Jake stood there with his hands on his hips and watched. He bit his lip. "I'm worried that you're not getting your complete nutrients."

Noah rolled his eyes. He did a lot of that since becoming a teenager. Where was his cherubic boy? Jake wondered. The one who was always laughing and smiling and used to make up his own knock-knock jokes? He must be somewhere inside that surly teenager.

"Dad, you were there when we met with the dietician. We went over everything." Noah straightened up, a package of tofu in his hand. "Mom's okay with it. Why can't you be?"

It was Jake's turn to roll his eyes. Sometimes, he wondered where Nadine's head was at. His ex-wife was too soft, he thought. He had to remind her she was the parent and not Noah's best friend. And being Nadine, she always bristled at that or any other kind of interference he tried to run. She had tried to encourage Noah into all sorts of art and music lessons while Jake was trying to get him involved with team sports. Neither had any success. The only thing Noah seemed to be interested in was his phone and his vegan diet.

"Have you had any blood work done?" Jake asked. "To make sure you're not deficient in any vitamins or minerals?"

"I have a physical once a year, okay?" Noah said. "Are we going to spend every day this summer talking about my diet? 'Cause if we are, then just send me home."

Jake threw his hands up in surrender. "All right. All right. But as your father, I am concerned about you."

"I'm fine."

Jake couldn't read the boy's expression because his messy mop of hair was in his eyes. He reached out and brushed it away. Noah reacted by jerking his head back. "Stop, Dad."

"Maybe it's time for a haircut," Jake said.

"Whatever," Noah grumbled.

Feeling unwelcome, Jake glanced at his watch. "I've got that call with your grandfather. Then I'm going to walk into town and grab a bite to eat."

"Did you want me to make you a Buddha bowl?"

Jake looked at all the ingredients laid out on the island. Half the stuff he couldn't identify. And what he could did not look appetizing at all. "No, that's all right. Don't go to any trouble." Changing the subject, he asked, "What are your plans for tonight?"

Noah shrugged, turning on the stove and putting some olive oil in a fry pan. "Might go down to the beach. Or take a walk around town."

"There's a tennis court on the other side of town. You should check that out."

When Noah said nothing, Jake added, "Don't stay out too late. And don't be on the beach or anywhere near the cliff's edge when it gets dark."

Noah rolled his eyes. Again.

The evenings lasted longer here, and dusk didn't happen until almost ten at night. Even so, Jake didn't want his son down at the beach at dark. Too many unknowns.

"Okay, I'll see you later."

There was an eight-hour time difference between Ireland and California. Jake hoped the call would be quick, as he wanted to head into town and pick up some takeout. Although here they called it takeaway. The food wasn't quite the same here: the pizza was a little different, and there were no chicken wings or tacos. But there were loaded fries. Fries smothered in garlic sauce and melted cheddar cheese or chili fries, which was fast becoming a guilty pleasure of his.

At the thought of guilty pleasures, an unbidden image of Maggie Moran floated before his eyes.

His laptop buzzed. His father.

"Good morning, Jake," Don Ballard barked as soon as the video call started. Jake didn't bother to point out that it was late afternoon in Ireland.

Like him and Noah, Jake's father had a thick head of hair, though his was now snow white. His skin was tanned from days spent golfing and making deals on the golf course or at the bar at the country club. Don Ballard was semi-retired and planned to hand off the business to Jake within a few years.

"How are things in Ireland?" Don asked. "How's Noah getting on?"

"We're fine, settling in," Jake said. "How's Mom?"

"You know your mother. She's busy making soup down at the city mission." Although Don wouldn't be caught dead making soup down at the city mission, he was proud of his wife's philanthropy and supported her.

"How's Jackie?" Jake enquired after his sister.

"She's fine," his father said, brightening up. "She's got a show this weekend at some gallery in Taos. Your mother and I are going down for it."

There was a pause before they got down to business.

"Well, where are we with this golf course?"

"I've got a meeting with someone from the planning authority in the morning," Jake said.

"Even though we haven't purchased the farm yet?"

"I've made a bid, but it's conditional on planning permission," Jake explained. His research had showed that planning permission in Ireland could be tricky, and there was no sense in owning the property if they wouldn't be allowed to build their golf course. Best to proceed with caution.

"And then what?"

"The application process will take a few weeks. So all we can do is wait," Jake said. It was a long, complex process.

"All right." Don sighed. "I don't suppose we could grease a few palms?"

Jake laughed. "Not a hope."

"All right, keep me posted," his father said.

ell

The next morning. Jake woke coughing and sneezing, indicating his seasonal allergies had kicked in. He thought he'd find a drugstore on the way to work, but then he remembered Maggie Moran owned a health food store and smiled to himself. It would be a good excuse to stop in and say hello.

After his run and a shower, he dressed for work and ate a quick breakfast of banana and a yogurt.

Noah sat on the sofa, his earbuds in and his gaze fixed on his phone. Jake wasn't sure if he was just getting up or if he'd been up all night.

"I'm going to work," Jake said. He sneezed.

Noah never looked up.

"It's okay, don't get up. Pay no attention to me, I'm just going to remove my clothes and walk through town in my birthday suit. That okay?" Still no response or acknowledgment. Jake sighed. "All right then," he muttered to himself.

His office was about a mile from the rental house, but the day was dry, and he walked. Every city he went to, every place he traveled to, he liked to explore on foot, even the side streets. It gave him a feel for the place he was visiting, and he liked to know a town well before he invested in it. He planned to do the same in the two months he was going to be in Ballygap.

The town curved down toward the sea, but he headed in the opposite direction, thinking he wouldn't mind a cup of coffee. He passed dress shops, a bookie, and the post office. People waved to him as he walked along the footpath.

There was a sign for a café down at the end of the row of shops that read, "The Sweet Tooth," and he picked up his pace and headed toward it. The smell of baked sugar wafted from the open door. That was enough of an enticement, but he hoped they served coffee as well.

The café was dimly lit, with floorboards the color of honey, mocha-colored walls, and a big slate blackboard behind the counter listing all the choices. The pastry case ran the width of the shop and featured many delectable offerings. Once the woman ahead of him completed her purchase, Jake stepped up to the counter, pulling his wallet out of his back pocket.

Behind the counter, a plus-sized blonde with a pretty smile greeted him. "Welcome to the Sweet Tooth. Can I help you?"

"I'd like a double-shot Americano with cream," Jake said.

"Anything else?" she asked with a glance at the pastry case.

"How about a muffin?" he asked.

"I've got blueberry, double chocolate chip, banana walnut, mixed berry—"

"Mixed berry, please," he said.

He paid for his order and the woman made his coffee and put a muffin on a plate for him. On the other side of the room, a display case was filled with an assortment of cakes.

"Do you make everything here? Or are the baked goods brought in?" Jake asked, curious.

"I make everything here myself from scratch," the woman said. She appeared to be in her early thirties.

"Are you the owner?"

"I am," she said, lifting her chin and smiling.

"That's great," he said. "I'm Jake, by the way."

"I'm Lily," she said with a smile.

He took the coffee and muffin from her and thanked her. He chose a seat in the front window so he could watch the people passing by outside. The coffee was hot and fresh. The muffin was an explosion of berries, and it delighted him to realize he'd just found his place for his morning coffee. It was nice to be settling in.

On the way out, he stopped at the counter and asked Lily, "Where's the health food store?"

"Right at the top of town. Head out the door, make a left, and it's about half a mile up the road."

"Thanks," Jake said.

Maggie's shop was easy to find and hard to miss. The small detached building was a bright shade of cobalt blue with white trim around the windows. A cheerful and quirky mural on one of the side walls depicted sunflowers, birds, and butterflies, and the words "Slainte Mhaith" were painted over the door in big, bright letters. He wouldn't dare try to pronounce that. The front door stood wide open.

Jake stepped across the threshold and looked around the inviting space with its varnished oak laminate floors. Oak shelving displayed a variety of products from herbal supplements to candles to books, and there was a mixed scent of lavender and mint and something else he couldn't identify. Music sounding like chimes played in the background. At the front of the shop was a small counter with a cash register and a card reader. Behind it, a girl of twenty or so regarded him as she sipped a hot brew from a china teacup.

"Well, hello there, welcome to Slainte Mhaith," she said. If quirky had a personification, this would be it, he thought. She wore a vest of colorful crocheted squares over a white T-shirt. Her fine blonde hair was in two little pigtails, and more studs lined her one outer ear than he could count in one glance. Her name tag read, "April."

"Can I help you?" she asked.

"I was looking for something for seasonal allergies," he replied.

She nodded and came out from behind the counter. "I can help you with that."

Jake followed her as she walked over to one of the shelves on the other side of the room.

"Depending on your symptoms, we have several items. If you've got sneezing, you could try this," she said, and she shoved a box into his hands. "Or if it's watery, itchy eyes, you could use these eyedrops." She stacked a small box on top of the one already in his hands. "And if it's blocked sinuses or something, you could always try a neti pot."

Neti pot? he wondered.

From the back of the shop, a female voice called, "April, did you call Mother Nature?"

Jake smiled to himself. He'd only met her once, but he'd recognize Maggie Moran's voice anywhere.

April looked at him, her shoulders hunched in, and her bottom lip dragged far right in an "uh-oh," kind of moment.

"You have Mother Nature's phone number?" Jake asked with a grin.

April nodded, still holding a neti pot in her hand. "Oh, sure, all the health food stores do," she said with a blank expression.

Jake went to open his mouth to retort but was interrupted when Maggie approached them.

A smile spread across her face. "Jake!"

"Good morning, Maggie," he said.

She'd piled her black hair up in a messy bun on top of her head. In the artificial light of the shop, light freckles were visible on her cheeks and nose, and her eyes appeared a darker blue, almost navy. Jake realized something: Maggie Moran was younger than he'd thought. He had to have at least ten years on her. It gave him pause. But only for a moment. He attempted a smile.

"You two know each other?" April interrupted. He'd forgotten she was there.

"Yes, we met the other day at the cliffs. Jake, this is my assistant, April. April, this is Jake Ballard. He's here on a working holiday," Maggie said with a smile.

Maggie lit up the room when she smiled. Jake wondered if she knew that.

"Oh, business and pleasure," April said.

"What brings you in here?" Maggie asked Jake.

Momentarily, he forgot why he had come into her shop. Maggie Moran was proving to be a pleasant distraction.

"Allergies," April said in a stage whisper.

"Oh, right," Maggie whispered back.

"Why are we whispering?" Jake asked, whispering as well.

April looked at him. "To give you a bit of privacy with your questions and purchase."

Jake didn't want to point out to the girl that they were the only ones in the shop. He looked at Maggie, who shrugged again and smiled.

Once April scanned his items, he paid for them with his credit card as she set them in a brown paper shopping bag. She handed it to him and smiled. "How long are you in Ballygap for?"

"The summer."

"That long?" she asked. She glanced over at Maggie, standing next to Jake. "You should get someone to show you around."

Jake laughed. "I should."

"Maggie could do it," April volunteered.

"I could show you around Ballygap," Maggie said at the same time.

He was about to protest, but he didn't want to give her a chance to back out of it. "Are you sure? I don't want to take you away from anything." He glanced around the shop.

"It's not a problem at all. We could do a walking tour," Maggie said.

"Sounds great."

"Might as well start now," April said.

Maggie blinked. "What?"

April stepped out from behind the counter, corralled the two of them, and herded them toward the door.

"Yeah, now's as good a time as any," April pressed. "It's quiet."

Jake exchanged a glance with Maggie and shrugged. "Shall we?"

Maggie gave him a tentative smile. "We shall."

CHAPTER THREE

MAGGIE STEPPED OUTSIDE WITH Jake following her. It felt odd to be stepping away from work during the day to show a fella around. Once they were outside, she looked down toward the town. She wanted to make the brief tour memorable. To be honest, she hoped he'd find her memorable.

"Where to first, Maggie?" he asked.

"Um, we could walk through town and head out toward the cliffs," she said. When he didn't respond, she added, "Unless of course you wanted to see something else, or maybe you have to be at work."

When Jake smiled at her, Maggie wanted to melt.

"Not yet. I'm open to any suggestions," he said.

"Do you mind if I ask what kind of business it is that you do?"

"Not at all. Our family company, Greystone Development, builds hotels, resorts, and golf courses all around the world. Last year, we built in Las Vegas and Dubai."

"Oh," Maggie said. She had not expected this. If a golf course was going to be built, it certainly wouldn't be in the middle of the town. She glanced up the road that led past the shop and out of town. There was farmland out that way for sale that had prime land.

"You seem disappointed," Jake said with a laugh.

"Oh no, it's just not what I expected," Maggie said.

Jake winked at her. "I hate disappointing a woman."

Maggie blushed. Jake's short sleeves revealed the ropey veins winding their way up his arms. She would have liked to reach over and trace them with her finger.

"Where to?" he prompted.

"Oh, right, sorry," Maggie said. She headed toward town with Jake at her side.

They hadn't walked far when Jake asked, "Would you mind switching places with me?"

She'd been walking on the side nearest the street. "No, not at all." They went to switch but bumped into each other. They tried again and the same thing happened.

They both laughed.

"You go first," Jake said. Maggie went on the inside and Jake stepped closer to the road. She thought it was peculiar but said nothing.

Maggie spent the next hour with Jake, walking around town. She decided not to take him out toward the sea, knowing he'd already seen the ocean and the cliffs. As they walked, she point-ed out former businesses that had closed down, highlighting the fact that the town needed investment. And commitment. When they passed townspeople, she introduced him to them. He was chatty, and Maggie thought that he'd fit right in in Ballygap. She showed him the only petrol station in town, the grocery store, and the butcher.

"Where's a good place to take my son?" he asked.

Maggie blinked. "How old is he?"

"Seventeen," Jake said. "He'll be here with me for the summer."

Between the resemblance and the accent, Jake had to be referring to the teenager who'd come into Maggie's shop the other day. She hesitated only briefly before asking, "Is your wife here as well?" She cast a sideways glance at him. There was no sense in crushing on a married man.

Jake grinned, and Maggie felt as if she'd been caught out.

"I'm divorced," he said.

She nodded. "What does your son like to do?" she asked, steering the conversation back to a less awkward topic.

Jake sighed. "Nothing to do with sports, that's for sure."

Maggie laughed. "That's all right. Where is it written that because you're a man you have to be interested in sports?"

Jake laughed. "Nowhere, I guess."

He didn't elaborate, so Maggie changed the subject. "There's the beach, of course. And if you take the road out of town by the shop, there is a stone circle about two or three kilometers out of town."

"A stone circle?" Jake asked.

Maggie nodded. "Like a mini version of Stonehenge."

"Really?"

"Yeah, really. There's also a farm that has a ring fort. You can see it from the road and take pictures. Which is just as well, because the fella that owns the farm doesn't welcome trespassers."

"Noted."

"Did you come into town from the Dublin side?" she asked.

"We did."

"Did you see those castle ruins on that high elevation?"

"Noah saw it."

"It's thought to be one of the oldest castle ruins in Ireland. There isn't much left of it. Only the tower. But the farmer who owns it will let you climb the hill to view it. There are some magnificent views. But you can pack a lunch, and it's worth the trip."

"Thanks."

The footpath was narrow and at times, their elbows brushed against each other. Not that Maggie was complaining. She was happy to be in his presence. She didn't want the tour to end, and for the first time in a long time, she wasn't anxious to get back to her shop.

Jake stopped when they arrived in front of a renovated building that appeared to be office space, next to a hair salon and a dress shop. "This is where I get off."

Maggie frowned, not understanding.

With a thumb pointing over his shoulder to the building behind him, Jake said, "This is my office space."

"Oh, oh, of course," Maggie said. They had to go back to work, whether or not she wanted to.

"Maggie, thanks for showing me around. I appreciate it."

"Not a problem," she said. "I'll see you around, Jake."

"Sure."

Maggie walked away, feeling a bit dejected.

"Maggie?" he called out after her.

"Yes?" she asked, turning around.

Jake rubbed the back of his head. "Can I take you to lunch on Friday?"

"You can." She smiled. It was only two days away. Surely the wait wouldn't kill her.

"I can pick you up at your shop, if that's all right."

Maggie nodded. "Sounds good."

He broke into a smile. "That's great. One o'clock?"

"Perfect. See you then, Jake!" she said. She turned and headed back to her shop, her step light and a smile on her face. It had been a long time since she'd had a serious crush on someone. And an even longer time since someone had asked her out on a date.

It was a date, wasn't it?

—— *ele* ——

When Maggie returned to her shop, she found April sitting on the high stool behind the counter, playing her ukulele. April stopped strumming and set the instrument down when Maggie walked through the door.

"So you're back then."

"It appears so," Maggie said with a smile.

"He's wicked fit, isn't he?" April said with a faraway expression on her face.

"He is," Maggie agreed.

April nodded. "Did you see his shoulders? And those biceps? I bet they're rock hard."

Maggie had noticed all those things; it was hard not to. She'd also noticed his sun-kissed skin and his grin. But most of all, she had noticed how she felt in his presence. Full of hope for all possible things.

"I wonder if he has a girlfriend," April mused, looking out the window, her ukulele forgotten.

"Isn't he a little old for you?" Maggie pointed out. Jake had to be twenty years older than her assistant.

April shrugged and smiled a dreamy smile. "So? There's something to be said for older men. They're more mature. More settled. They know what they want and what they don't. All that sowing their oats is way behind them."

Maggie scowled at her, even though she had to admit that she agreed. She knew there was nothing to be jealous about where April was concerned. April went wherever the wind blew her, and most likely, she would forget all about Jake as soon as the next man walked through the door and piqued her interest.

April stared out the window.

"Did you call the serviceman for the coffee machine?" Maggie asked.

April snapped her fingers. "That's what I meant to do. I'll do it now," she said, as if she'd come up with the idea herself.

Maggie headed back to her office, humming a tune. She glanced at the clock on the wall. She had a lot to do before closing time. But Jake Ballard was definitely on her mind.

CHAPTER FOUR

WHEN JAKE ARRIVED HOME from work, he found Noah tucked in the corner of the sofa, earbuds in, his eyes glued to his phone. Jake wondered if he'd left the house at all that day. He hadn't brought his son six thousand miles to a beautiful country so he could stay indoors and stare at a screen. Although he was irritated, he refused to let it put him in a bad mood. He was still on a high from Maggie agreeing to go out to lunch with him. That "yes" would certainly buoy him for the next few days until he met up with her. It was something he was definitely looking forward to.

Noah didn't look up when Jake entered, and Jake wondered if he even knew he was there. It gave him cause for alarm. If there was a break-in, would Noah even notice?

"Hey, how was your day?" Jake called out.

Noah didn't look up.

Jake walked over and pulled an earbud out of one ear.

Noah responded by jumping up off the sofa and scowling. "Hey, what did you do that for?"

"Because I'm home from work and I want to talk to you. I asked how your day was," Jake explained.

"It was fine," Noah said, heading to the kitchen. He pulled a glass down from a cabinet and the water pitcher from the fridge.

"What did you do all day?" Jake asked.

Noah shrugged, filling the glass.

"I thought we could go to a hurling match sometime. Apparently, it's the national sport, and I'd like to see what it's all about."

"Nah, I'm good," Noah said. He took a long gulp of his water.

"Wouldn't you be interested in seeing some of the different sports they play in Ireland?" Jake asked, hopeful.

"Nope."

He wished Noah would take an interest in sports; it would make his life so much easier. Even if he didn't want to play sports, there were all sorts of teams you could follow. The suggestions Maggie had made to him earlier came to mind, and Jake decided he'd try a different tack with his son.

"Maybe over the weekend, we could drive out and see some of the sights."

Noah snorted. "Whatever."

"There's a stone circle that's supposed to be ancient, like Stonehenge," Jake said.

There was a faint glimmer of interest in Noah's expression, but it disappeared quickly, and he returned his attention to his phone.

"There are some castle ruins, a ring fort," Jake said, not even sure what that was.

"Okay, calm down, Dad. We're here for the whole summer. We don't have to see everything in one weekend."

"All right, but don't make any plans for Saturday," Jake said.

Noah grunted, not looking up from his phone.

"Have you eaten dinner yet?" Jake asked.

"No."

"Why don't we go into town and grab something?" Jake suggested.

Noah looked up. "Cool, I'll be outside. I'm starving."

"Let me change and I'll be right out," Jake said.

When Jake headed outside, he noticed Noah sitting in the front seat of the car. He rapped on the window. "Come on, we can walk."

Noah got out of the car and slammed the door. "God, Dad, you really make things difficult. Why can't we drive? It's faster."

Before Jake could respond, the girl next door appeared from around the side of her house, wheeling her bike. She was about Noah's age, all red hair and freckles.

"Hi," she said.

Jake waved and Noah said, "Hi."

She stopped as she approached them and said to Noah, "We're all cycling up to the cliffs. Did you want to come with us?"

"Maybe another time," Noah said.

"Suit yourself," she said and waved. She cycled out of her driveway and headed out toward the cliffs and the ocean.

Jake and Noah were quiet for a moment, watching the girl ride away.

"I suppose you'll be wanting a bike while we're here," Jake said.

"Yeah, I think I would," Noah replied.

Jake whistled as he got ready for his lunch date with Maggie. He'd stopped at home after work to check on Noah and to freshen up. He'd been busy since he'd last seen her: The planning permission application had been filled out and lodged. There would be a notice printed in Ballygap's weekly paper, and a notice of intention would be signposted at McDougal farm along the cliffs.

At least the ball was rolling. Jake had met with two different architectural firms from Dublin, and they had discussed at length his plans and vision for the area.

But for now, with a small sense of accomplishment, he wanted to focus on Maggie. Since his divorce, he'd dated a few women but none that had held his interest. Plus, his job required a lot of travel, and that didn't leave a lot of time to pursue any relationships.

But Maggie was different. He knew that from the moment he'd met her. There wasn't one thing about Maggie Moran that he didn't like. She was a bit younger than him, but he'd decided he wasn't going to let that bother him.

She was waiting for him when he arrived at her shop. April was in the front of the store, unloading a box and stocking shelves.

"Have fun, you two," she said. She winked at them, and Jake watched as a lovely pink tinge fanned out across Maggie's cheeks.

As they walked out of the shop, Jake held the door open for her. Maggie had suggested a place at the edge of town. It was a ten-minute walk, but Jake didn't mind. It gave him a chance to study her in profile as she walked alongside him. The day was warmer than the ones previous, and that gave Jake hope that there might be an actual summer in Ireland. Maggie wore a maxi dress with a short bolero sweater. Her dark hair was swept up into a messy bun, and large gold hoop earrings dangled from her ears.

The staff at the little restaurant greeted Maggie by name and led them to a table in the front, in a section styled like a glass atrium. As they perused the menu, Jake said, "I see they have an extensive vegan selection."

Maggie lowered her menu to look at him, and Jake explained. "My son, Noah, has been a committed vegan for the past year."

"Good for him," Maggie said. "You know, I think I've met your son. There was an American boy who came into the shop for vegan snacks." She went on to describe him.

"That's him," Jake said proudly.

"He's the image of you." Maggie smiled.

"Thanks. I worry that he's not getting everything he needs with this diet of his." Jake said.

"Have you addressed your concerns with your GP and a nutritionist?" Maggie asked.

Jake nodded.

"Well then?"

"I'm still not convinced."

"There's a lot to be said for a plant-based diet," Maggie said.

Deciding that he didn't want Noah's diet to be the main topic of conversation, he changed the subject.

"Were you born and raised in Ballygap?" he asked.

She shook her head. The server came over, interrupting them, and took their order. Once he left, Maggie answered, "Actually, Dublin. My father was a mathematician and my mother taught at Trinity."

"How did you end up in Ballygap?"

A shadow crossed her face. "My parents were killed in a car crash when I was fifteen. I had to come here to live with my grandparents."

"I am so sorry," Jake said, wanting to kick himself for bringing up a painful subject.

Maggie shrugged and gave him a small smile. "It's all right. Don't worry about it."

"It must have been a painful period in your life."

Maggie's eyes darkened. "It was, but with the help of my grandparents, my Aunt Eileen, and some newfound friends, I managed to get through it."

"You never went back to Dublin?"

Maggie shook her head. "No. When I first arrived here, I used to tell myself that as soon as I turned eighteen, I would go back to Dublin and my life."

"But you changed your mind?"

"It turned out I had created a life for myself here. I love the town. It's my home." As they ate their lunch, she went on to tell him about the shop, how she taught a weekly tai chi class, and how she organized the annual Ballygap Fun Run to aid local charities.

"That will be happening soon, in case you're interested," she added. Before he could respond positively, she reddened and said, "I'm sorry, I've been talking only about myself."

"Don't be sorry," he said honestly. He could listen to her talk all afternoon. An image came to mind of the two of them together on a sofa on a Sunday morning, reading the newspapers, her leaning into him to read him something she found interesting or funny. Her voice was lyrical, and if she wanted to recite the phone book, he'd be interested in hearing it.

"How's Noah settling in?" Maggie asked, shifting to more neutral ground.

"He's well," he said.

"And his mother?" Maggie asked.

"Nadine's back in California," Jake said. "We've been divorced for almost ten years."

"Do you get along with her?" Maggie asked.

"Yes, we do get along, thankfully," he said. "We have a child together, so we make an effort to be amicable."

Maggie nodded.

"I'm trying to get him involved in some sports, even if he just went to a game," Jake confessed.

"Why is that so important to you?" Maggie asked.

Jake opened his mouth, closed it, hesitated, and then started again. "Sometimes it's hard to find a sense of belonging in high school. It's harder if you're a little different. I thought it might help. It hurts to see my kid left out."

"Is he left out?"

Jake pondered this and conceded, "I don't know. It's just a sense I get."

"Maybe he's not left out so much as he's trying to find his way or his tribe," she suggested. "He must be interested in something. Maybe all you need to do is support him in what he loves to do or what's important to him."

He wondered if she was speaking from personal experience.

"Tell me about yourself," Maggie prompted. "What do you do when you're not working?"

Jake thought for a moment. "Well, I do like to run. I like to read books, mainly non-fiction, and I love to travel. Because I work so much, I can usually only get away for a few days at a time. But it's fine, because I've seen a lot of California."

"Any favorite spots?"

"Yes. I love Sausalito, Monterey, and San Francisco."

"I'd love to see California someday," Maggie said thoughtfully.

"You should go! I would love to show you around," he said. He realized he'd spoken too soon, and both of them laughed nervously and looked at everything in the restaurant except each other.

They skipped dessert and headed out, Jake deciding he'd walk Maggie back to her shop.

When the shop came into view, Jake said, "Thanks for coming to lunch."

She turned and smiled at him. Her smile was like a warm beam of light. "I enjoyed myself."

"Maybe we could do it again?" he asked, emboldened.

"I'd like that."

"All right, then, that's settled," Jake said.

Maggie laughed. It sounded like a silvery peal. She headed toward her shop, but before going inside she looked over her shoulder and said, "I'll see you around, Jake."

With a two-finger salute, he turned and went back to work.

CHAPTER FIVE

M AGGIE FELT AS IF she were walking on a cloud for the rest of the day. After work, she hurried home to feed the animals and take them out for an hour's walk, always aware of the time as she was meeting up with her two best friends later that evening. They got together at least a couple of times a month. And when they weren't meeting up, they were texting or ringing each other.

They had agreed to meet at Lily's. Maggie walked to her friend's house, which was in a housing estate just outside of the town center. Lily had recently had a baby and was married to the town's new GP. She had just returned to work at her café, the Sweet Tooth, after maternity leave. Their other friend, Eimear, was already there.

"Sorry I'm late," Maggie said, breathless from her brisk walk. She looked around Lily's kitchen. It was contemporary in style, with sleek, glossy white cabinets, black appliances, and a black slate floor. The lights had been dimmed, giving the space a softer look.

"No worries," Lily said. She held her baby, Jack, in her arms, now six months old. He was fussing a bit and Lily rocked him gently. "I thought this little fella would be asleep by now. He's got another tooth coming in."

"Poor baby," Maggie said, and she leaned in and kissed the top of the little boy's head. "Where's Sam?"

Lily frowned. "He's on call tonight."

Maggie nodded and looked at Eimear, already sitting at the table with a bottle of beer in front of her. "How are you?"

"Doing great," Eimear responded. She wore her dark auburn hair cropped short and had no patience for makeup, perfectly comfortable with the smattering of freckles across her nose and cheeks. An electrician by trade, she sat there in her signature bib overalls and T-shirt, arms crossed over her chest. She came across as gruff but without a doubt, if Maggie were in trouble in the middle of the night, Eimear would be the first one she would call. And Eimear would be there, no questions asked.

As Maggie sat down, she said, "There'll be an organizational meeting for the fun run in a couple of weeks."

"We'll be there," Lily said, setting a bottle of wine down on the table. "Of course, I'll be pushing a pram this year." Lily was all blonde hair and blue eyes and what Nana used to call "pleasantly plump." Somehow, despite the fussy baby, Lily had managed to put out a cheese-and-olive board, open a few bottles of wine, and arrange a sweet tray. Maggie had brought crackers and seaweed pesto.

"That's all right," Maggie said as she spooned pesto onto some crackers and slid a plate toward Lily.

"Thanks. I love this stuff. It's addictive," Lily said, taking a bite of her cracker.

Eimear took a large swig from her beer bottle. "I suppose I'll be there."

Maggie grinned. This was Eimear's way. She dragged her feet about everything, but once you got her there, she was gold. At last year's fun run, she had stayed behind at the parish hall until the end, helping with the cleanup.

"I have news," Eimear announced.

Just as she said that, baby Jack roared.

"Well, all right there," Eimear said in response, in mock offense.

"I'm sorry," Lily said, repositioning the baby.

Maggie smiled reassuringly at her friend. "It's all right. He's only a baby, he's allowed to be fussy."

Eimear scowled and Maggie shot her a stern look.

Lily sputtered on, holding her baby against her shoulder and patting his back. "Ever since I went back to work, he seems out of sorts."

Eimear snorted. "He'll get used to it."

Maggie frowned at her. "May I hold him?"

Lily looked surprised. "You want to hold him? When he's like this?"

Maggie nodded. She stood up and Lily handed her the baby. He protested, but Maggie nestled him in the crook of her arm and rocked him, cooing, "Shh, shh."

What she wouldn't give for a baby of her own.

"How about we switch?" Lily asked. "I'll go live in your home for a few days and you stay here." She briefly put her head in her hands, then swept back a lock of blonde hair. "Just kidding. Not really."

Maggie looked at her. Why Lily would think her life was enviable boggled Maggie's mind. She envied them both.

"Is anyone interested in my news?" Eimear asked. She chugged from her beer again.

"Of course!" Lily said, helping herself to more seaweed pesto and crackers.

Maggie sauntered back toward the kitchen table, singing a soft lullaby. The baby's eyes were closing.

"Ben has asked me to marry him," Eimear announced.

"Oh, that's wonderful!" Lily exclaimed. The baby let out a little cry, and Lily clamped her hand over her mouth.

Maggie's eyes widened. "That's great news. How did that come about?"

Eimear frowned at Maggie as if she were dense. "He asked. I said yes."

Maggie rolled her eyes. Eimear's partner, Ben, had asked Eimear to marry him many times over the years.

"All right, what made you say yes this time?" Maggie tried.

Eimear pressed her lips together, then sighed. "I realized that I'm kind of a difficult person."

"No!" Lily said in mock protest.

Maggie and Lily had known Eimear since the three of them formed their own little tribe in secondary school, shortly after Maggie had first arrived in Ballygap. Eimear had been crotchety even back then. They were outsiders, all for different reasons, who had drifted together.

"I guess I love him," Eimear grumbled.

"Really?" Lily asked, feigning surprise.

"Of course I do," Eimear said. "Why do you think I've been with him for ten years?"

"Because he cooks?" Maggie asked. Eimear could live on burgers and chips for the rest of her life and be happy about it. But her boyfriend, a mason, liked to cook. And he was good at it, which meant that Eimear was getting variety in her diet.

Eimear looked at Lily and asked, "Are you with Sam because he can take your pulse?"

Lily giggled. "No, I'm with Sam because he raises my pulse on a regular basis." This led to laughter and guffaws from the three of them.

Maggie looked at her two best friends, happy for them both. They seemed settled. A feeling enveloped her. Not jealousy—she wasn't that type of person. Perhaps it was longing. An intense desire for what her best friends had: stable relationships, and for Lily, a baby. Maggie glanced at Jack, sound asleep in her arms. It didn't seem on the horizon. Jake came to mind suddenly, and she had to bite her lip to suppress a smile.

Lily sipped her wine. "Speaking of raising pulses, have either of you seen that dishy American that's landed here?"

Maggie's ears perked up, and she inched closer to the table, careful not to wake the baby.

Lily continued. "He comes into the café every morning for coffee."

"What does he say?" Maggie asked.

Eimear frowned. "What do you mean, what does he say? I'll tell you what he says. 'I'll have a double-shot Americano with cream.' That's what he says."

Lily burst out laughing. "That's exactly what he says."

Eimear smiled, and soon the three of them were laughing.

"He's handsome, isn't he?" Lily asked no one in particular. Maggie could see how Lily's confidence had grown since she'd met Sam. Before, she'd been so shy and tongue-tied around men. Now, secure in marriage and motherhood, she had a newfound confidence.

"He came into the shop," Maggie said. She didn't mention running into him on the footpath near the cliffs. Or that he'd taken her to lunch. There were some things she just wanted to keep for herself. If she kept it to herself, then it was special, wasn't it?

"And?" Lily asked, waiting. Expectant.

Maggie shrugged but could barely contain her smile. "And nothing. He was just browsing." It was a policy of hers never to talk about her customers or their purchases, thinking they deserved a modicum of privacy. And while she wanted to keep the conversation about him going, she wouldn't divulge what he had bought or the reason that had brought him in there in the first place. But thank God for allergies.

"What is he, a tourist or something?" Eimear scowled.

"No, he's a developer looking to invest in Ballygap."

"Why?" Eimear asked again.

Maggie looked at her friend. She loved her to bits, but did she always have to be so sour? She hoped Eimear could manage a smile on her wedding day.

Before Maggie could reply, Lily spoke up. "That would be great. There are eighteen shops that are closed. Any kind of investment would be welcome, especially in the town center."

"A rising tide lifts all boats," Eimear said.

"Exactly," Lily said. She looked at Maggie. "Do you know what kind of business he's looking to invest in? Is it a start-up or an existing business? Oh no, what if it's another bakery-café?" A flash of panic crossed Lily's features.

Maggie laughed. "Um, I guess he's looking to build a golf course."

Lily's shoulders sagged. "A golf course? I can't see how that would help."

Maggie shrugged. The conversation turned away from Jake Ballard and back to Eimear and her wedding plans.

As Maggie walked home in the late twilight, she wanted to hug herself. It had been a long time since she'd been in such a good mood. She was looking forward to seeing Jake Ballard again. It was going to be a brilliant summer.

—*ele*—

In the morning, Maggie headed out along the cliff walk with the dogs in tow. She couldn't find the cat, and so they went on without him. It had been late when Maggie arrived home the night before, and she ended up staying in bed longer than usual. She bypassed the beach, staying on the footpath that skirted the cliffs. The dogs ran ahead. She kept her eyes peeled for Jake, hopeful that she might run into him.

The split-rail fence of the adjoining farm came into view. It was the largest landholding around and had once belonged to the McDougals, neighbors of the Morans for generations. Maggie's property wasn't as extensive, but it had oceanfront and beach access, which was one of the many reasons she loved her home. Old Joe McDougal had died a bachelor, leaving his estate to a niece who worked as a missionary in Africa. She'd had it on the market for the last two years, but there had been no offers.

As Maggie approached, she noticed the familiar white placard of a planning permission application posted on one of the fenceposts. That was a good sign: there was finally a buyer for the farm. She stopped to inspect the notice. As she read the permit, her eyes widened in surprise at the words "Greystone Development." This was where Jake was planning on building his golf course? She stood there for a good minute, staring at the notice but not seeing it, letting it sink in. Especially how it would affect her. The image that came to mind was her dodging golf balls outside her home and the dogs getting hit.

She sighed and moved on. He hadn't mentioned where he was building, and she hadn't asked. Never in a million years did she think it was going to be right next door to her home.

Maggie decided her best course of action was to talk with Jake. She cut short her walk and turned around, the dogs following. She would stop in and see him before she went to work.

Chapter Six

J AKE HAD JUST LEFT the office of the local councilman, Tom Duffy. The councilman was as excited as Jake was about the development of a golf course and resort, and they'd agreed to hold a public forum for the townspeople. It was best to get the support of the residents right from the start. Jake was already drafting his presentation in his mind.

He picked up a cup of takeaway coffee from the Sweet Tooth and was walking toward his office when he spotted Maggie ahead of him. Rather than shout in the street, he picked up his pace until he'd almost caught up with her.

"Hey, Maggie," he said.

She turned around and when she made eye contact, Jake noted she wore a strange expression on her face. One he couldn't read.

He held up his coffee. "Can I get you one?" he asked. He'd be happy to head back and pick one up for her if she wanted. It seemed rude to be drinking a coffee in front of her when she didn't have one of her own.

"No, thank you. I was just coming to see you," she said. Even though she wasn't smiling, this admission buoyed Jake.

"Great, come on," he said. They walked side by side toward his rented office space. "I was wondering if you'd like to go to dinner. I know a little place up in Galway where the seafood is fresh."

Maggie looked around and mumbled, "I'll let you know."

"Is everything all right?" he asked, concerned.

She gave him a smile, but Jake wasn't convinced. "How's Noah?" she asked.

"He's fine," Jake said. They arrived at his office, and Jake unlocked the door and held it open for Maggie as she stepped inside.

He was curious as to what was going on. Maggie didn't seem her usual bright self: her eyes looked stormy. For a moment, he wondered if he had asked her out and forgotten, but nothing jogged his memory. Was she angry because he hadn't called her? It had only been the other day. Oh boy, he hoped she wasn't one of those clingy types.

He set his coffee cup down on the desk in the reception area, then turned and gave her his full attention. "What's up?" He drank in the sight of her: the faded jeans, the sandals, and the blue-and-purple paisley blouse tied in a knot at the waist.

"I have a question about your development." She folded her arms across her chest.

Jake relaxed. Was that all? He could certainly handle that. "Have a seat."

She sat down on the sofa, and he took the chair closest to her. He leaned forward, his elbows resting on his thighs.

"I understand you are in the process of buying the McDougal farm," she said.

He wondered what her interest was in this. "Dependent on planning permission, yes."

"That's a pretty big farm," she said.

Jake frowned in confusion. He did not know where this conversation was going.

"It is, yes, which is one of the things that make it perfect for the kind of development we're planning."

She nodded. "Can I ask how that will affect the homes and properties around it?"

"The properties to the north and south of the McDougal land will be purchased by Greystone," he answered. He smiled and added, "And Greystone plans to be generous."

The color drained from Maggie's face. She appeared almost dazed. For a moment, he wondered if he should call a doctor. He reached for her hand, but she pulled it back. Her eyebrows knitted together in a scowl as she said, "My home borders the property to the south."

It was Jake's turn to be dazed. He sat there for a moment—just a moment—his mouth agape, but he recovered.

As gently as possible, he repeated, "It is Greystone's intent with the purchase of the property to acquire all the properties adjoining it."

"Do I have any say in the matter?"

Jake hesitated, trying to figure out a way to say what he had to say diplomatically.

"I thought as much." Maggie stood up from the sofa and leveled her gaze at him. "Acquire? That's just a euphemism for 'steal.'"

Jake flinched and stood up and faced her. "Maggie, we can—"

She cut him off, her eyes ablaze and her mouth pinched. "My home is not for sale. Period." And she walked out the door.

There was no way the day was going to end without Jake seeing
Maggie and trying to talk to her about his development and her
home. He would outline the benefits for her in selling. He liked
her too much to just let it go. Too much to let a rift develop
between them.

Although he was friendly with everyone he'd met in Ballygap, he was not in a position yet to ask around for Maggie's
address. He rang the councilman, Tom Duffy, who was happy
to let him know which house was Maggie's. Jake glanced at
his watch. He assumed her shop closed at five like most of the
others in town, and he wanted to give her some time to get
home before he showed up at her door. He sent a text to Noah,
letting him know he was going to be late. At six, he turned off
the office lights, set the alarm, locked the door, and headed out
toward the cliffs.

It was still bright out and the evening sky was streaked with
shades of lavender, pink, and blue. He spotted her cottage with
its thatched roof in the distance, perched at the end of a bluff,
but not too near the cliff's edge. By the looks of it, it had been
there for centuries. The hand-plastered walls looked like they
had once been painted an apricot with white trim around the
windows, but the place desperately needed a touch-up. The
bright red enameled Dutch door stood in sharp contrast to
the faded walls; it must have been a recent addition. Its bright
color shone in the late afternoon sun. There were flower boxes
along the windowsills with pansies and dahlias, and on one side
of the home was a claw-footed bathtub that had been trans-
formed into a small garden. The overall feel was 1950. Jake

grinned. He hadn't expected this, and yet it fit perfectly with what he knew of Maggie so far. Both quirky and traditional.

He sighed. This was going to be a problem. The McDougal farm horseshoed around Maggie's cottage. He didn't see any way the golf course could go ahead without her property. She'd have to sell it.

As he neared Maggie's home, he caught sight of her coming up from the path on the beach. The dogs followed her, trotting along, wagging their tails. Over one arm she carried a wide, flat wicker basket.

"Maggie!" he called out with a smile. Rufus stopped and when he spotted Jake, he charged toward him. Jake laughed.

"Rufus, come back here," Maggie called after him.

Jake bent down to pet the dog. "Hey there, buddy, how are you?"

"Jake," she said as she approached, her demeanor stiff. She wasn't smiling. Jake thought this whole thing was ridiculous.

He followed her to the front door of her cottage and frowned when he noted the contents of her basket.

"Is that seaweed?" he asked.

"Yes," she replied.

"You've got enough of it there. What are you doing with it? Bathing in it?" he said with a laugh.

She stopped and turned around to face him.

"It's an all-purpose natural ingredient," she replied. "I make homemade skin care products, and I make a wicked seaweed pesto." She paused and lifted her chin. "And yes, I take seaweed baths from time to time. They're very therapeutic."

Seaweed pesto? He thought of cracking a joke but decided against it. He dared not say anything, not wanting her mood to go any further south.

Maggie opened her front door and the dogs ran inside. Then Rufus ran back out to Jake and circled him, tail wagging.

"Maggie, don't you lock your door when you leave your house?" Jake asked, leaning down to pet the dog. They remained outside, and he wondered if she would invite him in.

Maggie shook her head. "No. I wasn't gone that long."

"You should rethink that," he said. "I'd hate for anything to happen to you." He didn't think any woman should leave her door unlocked at all.

Maggie scoffed. "Are you concerned about me?"

Without hesitation, he nodded. "Of course I am."

A red flush creeped up Maggie's neck.

From the doorway of the cottage, Daisy watched the interaction between Jake and Rufus, tentative.

"He doesn't seem friendly," Jake said, nodding toward the Irish setter, who stayed close by Maggie's side.

"Daisy's a girl," Maggie said.

Jake nodded toward the dog. "Sorry, girl, didn't mean to offend your delicate sensibilities." He looked up at Maggie and smiled. What did it say about him that he was apologizing to a dog?

"Daisy was a rescue. Her owner abused her. A man."

"I wish I could reassure her that all men aren't jerks."

Maggie snorted and shook her head. "It's a waste of your time coming around here."

"Before we get ahead of ourselves here, let's talk," Jake said, running his hand through his hair. Greystone hadn't even got planning permission yet. Her freezing him out might be all for naught.

"May I come in?" he asked.

She walked through her door and left it open. It was as much of an invitation as Jake was going to get from her.

He followed her in, along with Rufus. Maggie set her basket of seaweed down on the table.

Jake looked around. It was a small space with a kitchen area and a sitting room centered around a large hearth. There was a salt lamp in the window and fresh-cut sunflowers in a crystal vase on the kitchen table. An antique blanket box sat in one corner, and a framed piece of embroidery hung on the wall, reading, *Wide is the door of the little cottage*. A faint smell of lavender lingered in the air, and he noticed dried lavender hanging from the ceiling. Next to the door was an antique barometer.

She had her back to him and was filling a kettle with water.

"You have a lovely home," he said.

A loud crash sounded from a room off the sitting room. Startled, Jake raised his eyebrows and glanced in the direction the noise had come from.

"Oh, Twinkle!" Maggie said. She wiped her hands on a tea towel and said, "Excuse me."

She wasn't gone long before returning to the kitchen.

"Everything all right?" Jake asked.

Maggie nodded. "It's my cat. He has a bad habit of knocking things over."

Her attitude had definitely shifted. She wasn't the warm, bright Maggie he was growing used to. She was cordial but cool. He watched as she opened a canister and spooned loose tea into an infuser. There was going to be no offer of tea for him. That was all right. He had a tough exterior.

"It feels like a polar front has moved in," Jake teased.

Maggie turned around to face him. "Huh?"

"Never mind." When she said nothing, just went about the business of making herself a cup of tea, Jake said, "Look, can we talk about this?" He noticed the dogs had curled up on the sofa.

She looked up. "Talk about it? Why?"

"Because I think you may be getting ahead of yourself," Jake said. He stood there with his hands on his hips.

"Am I? We are talking about my home here," she said, raising her voice. The kettle boiled, clicked off, and Maggie poured water into her mug.

"Hold on, Maggie. Greystone hasn't got planning permission yet."

"*Yet*," Maggie repeated.

Jake sighed. He liked Maggie a lot, and he wanted to keep the door open between them for his own personal interest. "Look, Maggie, I don't want to be at odds over something that might not happen."

"But *if* planning permission were obtained, Greystone intends to take over the adjoining properties. No?" She stared at him, her blue eyes wide and—wary.

"But you'd be able to do anything you want with the compensation," he pointed out.

"Not true," she scoffed. "Not if what I really wanted was to keep my home."

Jake didn't know what to say, and he felt like he was grasping at straws.

Maggie sat down at the table with her mug of tea.

"May I sit down?" he asked.

"Suit yourself."

So much for Irish hospitality, he thought. He pulled out the chair across from her, thinking that any closer and she might protest. It was best to keep his distance while he tried to drive his point home.

"Is it always Greystone's practice to buy adjoining properties?" she asked.

"Yes," he said, unflinching. There was no point in lying. He'd be honest with her. He'd always purchased the adjoining properties as a buffer zone.

"So everywhere you go, you strong-arm people into selling their homes?" she asked.

"Greystone doesn't strong-arm anyone, I can assure you," Jake said.

"You, Greystone, it's the same thing," Maggie said. She looked at him.

He sighed. "Look, Maggie, I like you. A lot."

She widened her eyes and said, "So?"

"I would personally make sure your deal was fair and that you were well compensated."

"You're not listening, Jake. I'm not selling." Maggie enunciated each word for emphasis.

"But you could rebuild somewhere else. Anywhere else," Jake pointed out.

It surprised him when tears filled her eyes.

"I'm an eighth-generation Moran to live in this house," she said, lifting her chin as she spoke. "The Morans have lived here for over three hundred years. The remains of my great-great-grandfather's currach are still down on the beach."

Jake didn't know what to say to that. He wished Greystone didn't have to purchase her property, but because of the way the McDougal farm circled it, the purchase of Maggie's home would be compulsory.

He stood up from the table. There wasn't anything more to say. Maggie looked as deflated as he felt. "I should go," he said. Maggie didn't protest. Even Rufus didn't so much as lift his head as Jake walked toward the front door. Jake paused with his hand on the doorknob and looked back at Maggie.

"I am sorry, Maggie. But it's nothing personal. It's only business," Jake said.

CHAPTER SEVEN

M AGGIE ARRIVED AT THE parish hall for the town meeting just as it was about to start. There had been an announcement in the Ballygap weekly paper, and notices had been posted throughout town. By the look of the packed house, it seemed as if almost everyone was there. The place buzzed with excited conversation. But Maggie wasn't feeling it.

Her Aunt Eileen waved from the third row of chairs. Eileen sat with Olive Enright, one of the town's oldest residents, who was sharper than most of her younger counterparts.

Maggie said hello to both and took a seat next to her aunt. At sixty, her aunt had a vitality that made her beautiful. It was something that shone from within. Maggie was pretty sure other people noticed it as well. Now retired, Eileen was active in her community, volunteering and taking care of her own physical health.

Maggie nodded to the people around her, recognizing all of them. Small snippets of conversation surrounded her.

"How are you, Maggie?" her aunt asked. Eileen was her father's sister and was her only relative in Ballygap if you didn't count all the dead ones in the local cemetery.

"I'm well. Anxious to see what they have to say," she replied with a nod toward the front of the room.

"Same here," her aunt said.

"How've you been, Olive?" Maggie asked.

Olive was a petite woman with snow-white hair expertly coiffed and large eyes behind even larger glasses, with a beak-like nose and diaphanous skin that seemed to showcase every vein.

"If it weren't for my aches and pains, I'd be a lonely woman!" she said.

Maggie laughed. She couldn't wait to see the older woman's reaction to the proposed development. Olive was an active environmentalist. It wasn't just talk with Olive; the roof of her house had been retrofitted with solar panels, and she collected rainwater in a barrel for watering her extensive garden. She'd had her boiler replaced with electric heat, and she'd traded in her old car for an electric one. Not that she used it that much. Her preferred mode of transportation was walking. She'd given up her bike at eighty-five after almost being knocked down by a car.

Tom Duffy appeared at the front of the room along with Jake, who was smiling and appeared at ease as the two men conversed. Maggie's heart fluttered at the sight of Jake. The white business shirt he wore with his gray trousers made a striking contrast with his tanned skin. His hair was damp and his face clean-shaven.

As if reading her mind, Aunt Eileen said, "The American looks like a film star."

It had been three days since Jake had been at Maggie's house. She hadn't seen him around town or running along the footpath near the cliffs. She hated the fact that she looked for him everywhere she went, but it was like she couldn't help herself.

After he left her house the other night, she had wanted to curse the silence with relief. While he'd been inside, she had to admit she liked the way he looked in it despite their angry exchange. She imagined sitting on the sofa with him in front of a roaring fire while the wind blew and the rain pelted against the roof. Her mind had wandered to the two of them sharing a meal at her little wooden kitchen table. Of all the men to fall for! How impossible was that? The less she saw or interacted with Jake Ballard, the better. But saying and doing were two very different things.

Maggie caught sight of Lily at the back of the assembly, wheeling around the pram. She waved and returned her attention to the front of the hall.

Tom stood behind a podium, facing the crowd. Tom was Ballygap-born and bred, starting out as a dairy farmer but now keeping only dry cattle since becoming a member of council. He was a short man with jet-black hair that he dyed at home, which made it look like he'd used shoe polish on his head.

At the front of the room, Tom held court, bouncing from foot to foot as he spoke to the townspeople who approached him and introduced them to Jake. Finally, he pulled down a white screen from the ceiling, powered up a laptop for the presentation, and called the meeting to order.

"I've got some exciting news for you all and for the town of Ballygap," he started.

Maggie frowned. She'd never seen Tom so exuberant. You'd almost think that their syndicate's numbers had come in on the EuroMillions.

Once Tom dispensed with all the pleasantries, he proceeded with the meeting. "You all know the McDougal property."

The crowd in the parish hall hushed. Rumors had been floating around the community for the last few days. Everyone knew that Jake Ballard was there to invest money in Ballygap and that there was to be some kind of development with the McDougal property. Maggie sat up straighter and paid attention. A quick glance around the room showed that everyone else had, as well. She wondered if they would react to all the sordid details like she had. Despite the excited twitter that spread through the crowd, Maggie held her breath.

"I'm excited to say that the Greystone Corporation is seeking to purchase the property to build a world-class five-star resort and golf course," Tom said.

Maggie chewed on her lip and frowned. A five-star resort in addition to the golf course? This project was going to be bigger than she'd originally thought.

The councilor whipped a black sheet off of an easel, revealing a large poster board with pictures depicting pencil and watercolor drawings of a resort and golf course. Maggie wondered how much it cost to produce those vivid poster boards. A lot of money, she imagined. Going from left to right, she scanned the various placards on easels, looking at the artist's rendering of the proposed development and feeling sick at the image of a manicured fairway where her three-hundred-year-old cottage should be.

Eileen whispered in her ear, "This doesn't bode well for you."

"No, it doesn't."

While the rest of the crowd oohed and aahed, Maggie blinked back tears and tried not to slouch in her seat. It felt like a decision about her home had already been made, over which she had no control. Looking again at the placards on the easels, she pictured her home being bulldozed. Bile rose in her throat.

Tom continued, "Let me introduce you to Jake Ballard, from the Greystone Development Company out of California."

Maggie watched from her seat in the third row as Jake went through a presentation that made the golf course and resort sound like *the* must-have Christmas present for that year for the residents of Ballygap. Tom and Jake went through the various stages of the process from obtaining initial planning permission from the county council to all the studies that would need to be carried out, to final approval from An Bord Pleanála. If approval was granted, development would begin. Jake saved the best bit for last: how many jobs it would mean for the town and the surrounding area as well as the revenue generated for local businesses as resort guests explored the area.

Jake was a natural speaker, articulate and engaging. He seemed to ooze California sunshine and a lifestyle of ease. Maggie glanced around the community center. The audience sat there, quiet, their attention rapt. Several women had a glazed-over look to their facial expressions, and Maggie looked back to Jake at the front of the room and realized she wasn't the only one who found him attractive. By the looks of it, he could have sold them a swamp in Florida. But there weren't many jobs to be had in this part of the country, and the prospect of employment alone would be enough to sell the development plan. With a sinking feeling, she knew that this project would get the endorsement of the county council, the town's newspaper, and the townspeople themselves. And she couldn't blame them. Her life as she knew it—the life she had cultivated since her arrival in Ballygap fifteen years ago—would come to an end. No matter what, she wasn't just going to step aside. She was going to fight for her home.

After their joint presentation, Tom Duffy opened the floor to questions.

One after another, townspeople stood up to voice their thoughts. The questions ranged from how many jobs there would be to when the hiring would start to how long it would take to build the resort. But not all were excited about the development. A farmer in the back, who was a good six feet tall, stood, wearing muddy jeans and wellies, and enquired about access to the secondary roads near the McDougal farm for heavy construction machinery and equipment. He did not seem happy about the prospect of the access roads needing to be built or the noise that would accompany the heavy machinery moving in and out. Maggie waited for someone to ask about the adjoining properties to the proposed golf course and what would happen to them, but that question never came.

Olive stood, and the rest of the people in the row stood up to let her out to the aisle so she could speak. Maggie decided she might as well follow her, because she wasn't going to let this meeting end until she got her question answered.

Ahead of her, Olive asked, "What impact will this have on the environment?"

Jake went to answer, but Tom took over. "All the necessary environmental impact studies will be conducted. I can assure you, Olive, that not one shovelful of dirt will be upturned until all environmental studies are concluded."

Olive seemed satisfied, but Maggie knew Olive would ring Tom's constituency office first thing in the morning to discuss the matter further. Olive returned to her seat.

Maggie stepped up to the mic, realizing all eyes were on her, including Jake's. Her neck felt hot, and she focused on a spot straight ahead on the wall behind Tom.

"Will you please explain what impact this development will have on those people whose properties border the McDougal farm?"

Tom looked over at Jake. "Do you want to take this one?"

Jake did not hesitate. "I'll be blunt. We hope to make an offer of purchase on those properties—"

A murmur spread like a wave through the crowd, and Jake added, raising his voice, "And Greystone Development will offer above market value."

Jake flashed Maggie an entreating look, but she steeled her body against any kind of response. He looked to her just then like a man who was used to getting his way, and who used charm as a weapon in his arsenal.

"And what if someone doesn't want to sell their property?" Maggie asked. She wanted an answer to this.

Jake looked at Maggie as he replied, "In a case like that, we'd want to work one on one to find a way forward that's in the interest of both the homeowner and Greystone, an outcome that would be mutually beneficial to both."

"Thank you," Maggie muttered, not looking at him. She returned to her seat. As she did, she glanced over at Peg O'Malley, a neighbor on the other side of the McDougal farm. Peg was retired, having given up dairy farming after the death of her husband. She was all smiles. Everyone in town knew her fantasy was to live in Spain. This would be a dream come true for Peg. She was probably sitting in her seat pinching herself.

Maggie swallowed hard. Selling her home was not an option. She had planned to spend the rest of her life—however long or short it might be—in that cottage on the bluff overlooking the sea, the same way her grandparents had. Her stomach clenched at the possibility that she might lose it. That she might be steamrolled over in an American developer's plans. She felt dizzy, and small beads of perspiration appeared on her brow.

Jake spoke. "I will be in contact with those property owners over the next few days. Like I said, we hope everyone in the town of Ballygap will be on board when they recognize the value of such a development going forward. I realize there will be a couple of outliers, as nothing is one hundred percent, but I would like the opportunity to talk with every individual."

Her heart sank for the umpteenth time that night. Not only would she have to go up against this American company, but it would also put her at odds with her community. She hoped it wouldn't affect her business, but she suspected it would. People could be funny.

Maggie sat back down in her seat and gathered her poncho and satchel, waiting for the whole thing to be over so she could go home and figure out what to do next. Eileen patted her hand. "Don't worry, he hasn't built his golf course yet. You still have your home."

But for how long? she wondered. She didn't like all this uncertainty hanging over her head.

As the meeting closed, Maggie stood up. Olive reached out to her, aghast.

"Maggie, I'm so sorry your home is under threat. You have my support, of course."

Maggie nodded, bid them goodbye, and slipped out of the row of seats.

She glanced over her shoulder and saw Jake swarmed by townspeople. He stood a head above the crowd. Maggie headed out of the parish hall, numb. She wondered what her grandparents would have thought about all of this. There was a part of her that was glad they weren't alive to experience the singular, gut-wrenching heartache this would have caused them.

She looked around the town, at the people walking up and down the footpaths, people pouring out of the parish hall, and realized she had never felt so alone since the day she arrived in Ballygap. And that was an awful feeling she cared not to relive.

The sun began its descent on the western horizon of the Atlantic as she headed home. As her cottage grew closer, so did the spread that was the McDougal farm. Endless grassland for as far as the eye could see. It would make an excellent resort and golf course. But there was no way Maggie was giving up her home just to make it so.

The death of her parents had shattered her, but she'd found solace in the home of her grandparents and the little town, growing so attached to the place that even after finishing college, she'd wanted to return and make her life there. Over the years, she'd watched as other people left for other parts of the country or destinations abroad, but she'd always been happy living in Ballygap.

～ℓℓ～

Feeling an anxiety that wouldn't abate even after a hot bath and some deep-breathing exercises, Maggie pulled her cream-colored cable stitch poncho off the rocker in the corner, threw it on over her T-shirt and jeans, and headed out with the dogs. Rufus carried Twinkle by the scruff of his neck.

She had realized long ago that she'd always need to be near water, whether it be an ocean or a lake. The sea was the home of her soul. She never tired of the beach or the surf. Even in the dead of winter, when the gusts buffeted the coast and her little cottage and it was too dangerous to let the cat out of the house, Maggie still loved it.

Daisy walked alongside Maggie. Once Rufus dropped the cat on the path, he ran on ahead, barking at nothing in particular. She must keep busy and distracted. Keeping busy and distracted had proved to be a coping mechanism since she landed in Ballygap. In her first days there, Nana had kept her so busy she hadn't had time to think about things.

Once they arrived on the beach, Maggie found a place to sit, and the dogs headed for the surf. Daisy loved the water and within minutes, both she and Rufus were in up to their heads. Twinkle walked around, sniffing at things, periodically glancing at the two dogs in the water with what appeared to be a look of disdain.

The sea was dark gray, but the sky was the color of the palest lavender. June was a pleasant month. It meant a longer stretch in the evenings, and by five in the morning the sky was light, and the birds were singing.

Maggie's throat felt heavy and constricted at the same time, while her eyes felt moist. *I just have to get through this moment and come out the other side*, she told herself as she had thousands of times before.

She felt the sting of unshed tears but stared out to sea and swallowed hard. There were no boats anywhere. This cove was quiet, and once in a while she would have liked to see a boat or a freighter. Then maybe she wouldn't feel so alone.

The dogs, their fur soaked and smelling of seawater, came running toward her. Daisy panted, and Rufus waited until he was just in front of Maggie before shaking the water from his coat. Despite leaning back and putting her hands up, Maggie was sprayed with ocean water.

"Thanks," she said drily.

Rufus observed her, his tongue hanging out and tail wagging. Daisy sniffed something in the sand.

Distracted, Maggie stood up and brushed sand off the seat of her pants.

"Are we ready?" she asked.

Rufus barked and Daisy wagged her tail. The cat was already heading toward the path.

She thought of her ancestors who had lived in the cottage before her and how the men walked down this same path for generations to take their currachs out for fishing. Her great-great-great-grandfather and his brother had drowned out there in the Atlantic, one of their bodies washing ashore months later. In the nineteenth century, fishermen were identified by their cable knit sweaters. Each family had their own pattern. Maggie never failed to think about this when she came down here, how her family had made a living off the sea for centuries, and how all the old ways had died with the past. She looked again at the remains of the last currach of her family. It might be the only thing that remained as a testament to her heritage.

Her ancestors were most likely rolling in their graves at the thought of the homeplace being flattened for a golf course.

CHAPTER EIGHT

J AKE WAS MOSTLY PLEASED as he reflected on the town meeting and the turnout. The residents seemed enthusiastic about the prospective development. The only cloud on the horizon was Maggie and her home. Of all the homes that could stand in the way of his project, it had to be hers. Sometimes fate was a cruel mistress. But, he decided, it didn't have to be. Maybe Maggie didn't want to see him, but he was going to see her. He liked her. And he thought, given time, he could get her to see his way of thinking. But he needed to keep the lines of communication open. And that would be impossible if they didn't see each other. He'd give her a few days to settle down before he approached her again.

Noah rolled in to the kitchen, hair all over the place, wearing a T-shirt and boxers.

"What time did you go to bed last night?" Jake asked.

Noah shrugged. "I dunno. It was late."

"Did you do your chores yesterday?" Jake asked.

Noah sighed as if he couldn't be bothered. "I'll do them today."

"Noah, this is the third day I'm asking you to do some chores. I can't do it all myself," Jake said, exasperated. He made a mental note to ask Nadine if Noah was like this at home.

"I'll do it. Stop nagging me," Noah said.

"Don't go anywhere until the chores are finished," Jake warned.

Noah said nothing and Jake asked, "When's the last time you Skyped your mother?"

The boy stopped what he was doing and looked up. "Three or four days ago."

"Do that today, as well," Jake said. "In fact, you might as well tell your friend from next door—"

"Her name's Roisin."

"Okay, fine. You might as well tell Roisin you won't see her until tomorrow."

"Ha-ha, Dad," Noah said with a roll of his eyes.

As Jake headed out the door, he said, "And I hope you haven't made any plans for Saturday, because you and I are going sightseeing."

He closed the door just as Noah groaned, "Oh, man!"

———*ℓℓ*———

After lunch, Jake had a brief video conversation with his father. His dad was up early as he had a tee-off at dawn.

"Well, how did it go?" Don demanded, once his face came into view.

"It went very well," Jake said. He summed up the meeting and the nature of the questions. Thinking of Maggie, he added, "There are a few holdouts."

"What do you mean?"

"There's at least one person who doesn't want to sell their land to Greystone," Jake said.

"Is their property necessary?"

Jake nodded. "Yes, it's surrounded on three sides by the McDougal farm."

His father frowned, deep lines etching his tanned forehead. "Why don't they want to sell?"

"Sentimental value."

"That's hogwash," Don scoffed. "Offer them generous reimbursement, but not too much or we'll look like desperate fools. And if that doesn't work, get the piece of land through legal channels. Eminent domain. Compulsory purchase order or whatever legal term they use in Ireland."

Jake pressed his lips together in a thin line. The last thing he wanted to do was take Maggie's property—or anyone's property—through the courts. That would leave an unpleasant taste in everyone's mouth. Even his.

"I'll get legal to give us the name of a firm in Dublin," Don said.

Before Jake could protest, his father said, "I've got to go. My golf game awaits." And he signed off.

─────ele─────

Early Saturday morning, Jake rousted Noah out of bed.

"Come on, let's go, get up," Jake said, shaking Noah's foot.

This elicited a groan and a mumbling. "Don't you have to go to work?"

"Not today, I've got plans for us today," Jake said. He stepped over to the window and pulled the cord for the drapes, opening them. Bright sunshine spilled through the room.

"*Argh*," Noah groaned, pulling the sheet over his head.

"I'll get your breakfast ready," Jake said. "Be dressed and out in the kitchen in ten minutes."

"I have plans today, Dad," Noah said.

"I know you do. With me," Jake said. "Ten minutes."

It was more like fifteen minutes before Noah arrived in the kitchen, which was fine as Jake was just spreading mashed avocado over two pieces of whole wheat toast. He sprinkled a little black pepper over it and handed the plate to Noah as he passed by.

Noah grunted a "thanks" and took the plate over to the kitchen table. Jake poured a tall glass of orange juice and set it down in front of his son.

"Why do we have to get up so early?" Noah asked.

"Because we're going to make a day of it," Jake said. "I've got a few things around here I'd like to see, but I thought today we could drive over and visit that site, Newgrange." Noah had mentioned it a couple of times.

"Newgrange?" Noah repeated. "Isn't that on the other side of the country?"

"It is. It's over in County Meath. I thought if we got an early start, we could get there by the time it opened and not be rushed," Jake said. "We could stop for lunch. You can pick the restaurant."

"It's just that it's so early," Noah protested.

"The sun's up and the farmers are up," Jake said.

Noah scowled at him. "The farmers are up? What does that have to do with anything?"

Jake shrugged. He'd heard several tractors going by already that morning.

It didn't take long for Noah to get his things together and get out to the car. But if Jake had expected some conversation on the three-hour drive, he was mistaken. As soon as he pulled his rental car out of the drive, Noah was powering up his phone and putting his earbuds in.

Jake settled back in his seat, determined not to let any thoughts of Maggie, her home, or his golf course invade his thoughts and ruin his day. He occupied his mind with the scenery, which was beautiful. Bucolic. He'd never seen so many shades of green. The constant stream of rolling pastures and gentle hills dotted with sheep and cows never grew old. He found it relaxing and preferable to the traffic gridlock he encountered back home in California.

They were half an hour from their destination when Noah removed his earbuds and said, "Do you see the car ahead of us?"

"Yep."

"See how the first part of the license plate reads one-nine-one dash L-K followed by more numbers?"

"I do," Jake said.

"That means the car was bought in the first half of 2019 and registered in County Limerick."

"Interesting."

"Look over there—that car is from 2006 and it's from Dublin," Noah pointed out.

"Where did you learn that?"

"Roisin told me," he said.

"So your trip to Ireland hasn't been a total waste," Jake teased.

"Dad," Noah said, turning to look out the window.

Noah had been spending a lot of time with Roisin. Jake was glad that he had made a friend. Since Noah had gotten his bike, he and Roisin cycled everywhere around Ballygap every day, sometimes with friends of Roisin's. Jake was glad he wasn't stuck inside the house, staring at a screen all day.

Proceeding with caution, Jake said, "She seems like a nice girl."

This elicited a shrug from Noah. "Yeah."

Jake opted to drop the subject, not wanting to ruin their day. He figured if Noah wanted him to know something about her, he'd tell him. Jake had met her parents, and they were nice people. They had told him that if he or Noah needed anything, just to let them know. Also, they'd said that Noah was a gentleman, and Roisin's father had said that Noah was pretty articulate for a teenager. That moment had made Jake proud. Despite everything, maybe he and Nadine were doing something right.

Noah looked at his phone and said, "Did you know Newgrange is older than Stonehenge and the pyramids of Egypt?"

"I did not. Tell me more," Jake prompted.

Noah rattled off facts about the ancient site. "It's a UNESCO World Heritage Site. It's two hundred and seventy-nine feet in diameter and forty-three feet in height. The area covers an acre."

Jake had made the right choice dragging Noah out of bed at the crack of dawn. The kid was excited to see this place. Jake listened as his son continued to tell him about Newgrange.

Jake found his way to the visitor center and parked the car. He and Noah headed in to purchase tickets for the tour.

The tour guide explained facts about Newgrange, and Noah kept looking at his father and shaking his head in awe. As they neared the monument, their mouths fell open.

Noah said what Jake felt. "Wow!"

In front of them was a large dome-shaped structure. It was encircled with stone, but the dome-shaped mound was covered in grass. The stones in front of the entrance were carved with spiral designs.

The small group followed the tour guide into the inner chamber, with Jake and Noah bringing up the rear. The inner sanctum was comprised of large stones. It was low, long, and narrow. As Jake edged in, his shoulders pushed up against the walls of the chamber. It wouldn't be for those who were claustrophobic, Jake thought to himself. The guide explained to the group how the sunlight shone through the interior at the winter solstice, provided the sun was out. The guide also explained that there was a lottery every year, and those who got picked could go inside the chamber during the solstice. They got upwards of thirty thousand applications annually.

Noah, who was standing in front of Jake, said, "That would be so cool!"

Jake agreed.

They spent the rest of the afternoon at the site, finishing up by strolling through the gift shop, where Noah picked up a souvenir for his mother. Afterward, they headed out in search of a late lunch. Noah did an online search and found a vegan restaurant about half an hour's drive away. Although Jake would have liked nothing more than a burger, he agreed to it and they went for some food. Throughout the meal, Noah was chatty. Jake decided not to mention sports or Noah's diet.

On the ride back to Ballygap, Noah said, "Gram and Gramp asked me if I'd like to go to France with them next year over Easter vacation."

Jake's head snapped in Noah's direction.

"When were you talking to Gram and Gramp?" And why didn't he know this?

"We've been emailing back and forth."

"Since when?" Jake asked.

"I emailed Gram to ask her if she had any Irish ancestry," Noah said. "She said all her ancestors were from France, which is cool, but that Gramp's mother was Irish. They both write in the email, and you can always tell Gramp's part because he types in all caps! It's like he's shouting or something."

"Are you emailing them regularly?" Jake asked, intrigued. He was all for Noah having a good relationship with his grand-parents.

Noah shrugged. "I guess. Gram's hilarious in her emails. She tells me all the funny stuff Gramp does that he doesn't even know he's doing. You'd never know he ran a multi-mil-lion-dollar business." Noah laughed.

"Like what?"

"Gramp practices his golf swing in the house even though he's not supposed to and last week, he ended up breaking an expensive vase." Noah shook his head in disbelief, a broad smile on his young face.

They went silent as Jake tried to process this recent informa-tion.

"You're smiling like an eejit," Noah said.

"An eejit?"

"Yeah, Roisin said that's what the Irish call idiots," Noah said with a laugh. "Dad, do you think Mom will let me go to France with Gram and Gramp?"

"I don't know, but I'll talk to her about it. I think it's a great idea."

The day had been a great success. Jake had had time to spend with Noah, and he was able to push Maggie and the development far from his mind.

CHAPTER NINE

OVER THE WEEKEND, MAGGIE met up with Lily and Eimear to go walking along the cliffs. They met at Lily's house. It was a beautiful day for a walk: the sun was shining and there was no breeze.

Lily's husband, Sam, answered the door. He had baby Jack in his arms. The baby was drooling all over his bib.

"Hey, Maggie, come on in, Eimear is already here," Sam said. He held the door open for her.

"Hi, Sam."

There was something very appealing about a man holding a baby, Maggie thought. She remembered when Sam Rooney had first arrived in Ballygap three years ago to replace Dr. Tobin, who had retired. Sam was a rare breed: he had the looks of a film star with his thick black hair and blue eyes, and he was kind. It wasn't long before they had christened him Swoony Rooney. It seemed as if every woman in town needed to see the doctor. But in the end, it was Lily who'd won his heart.

Maggie followed Sam inside, making funny faces to the baby, who looked at her over his father's shoulder. The baby giggled and Maggie smiled.

"My bride's upstairs trying to find something to wear. I keep telling her she looks great in anything, but she doesn't listen," he said, shaking his head.

Maggie and Eimear looked at each other and smiled. Lily had always been sensitive about her weight growing up, but Sam was trying to help her with that. And Maggie thought he was succeeding. Since her marriage, Lily had bloomed.

Lily came bounding down the stairs, breathless. "Oh, Maggie, Eimear, I'm sorry to keep you waiting."

"No worries," Eimear said. She glanced at her Fitbit and said, "Let's get going, though. Don't want to make a day of it."

"Why? Going home to look through bridal magazines?" Maggie teased.

Eimear scowled at her. Lily glanced at her two friends and giggled.

As the three of them headed out the door, Lily said to Sam, "I won't be long. Just going for a walk. Then we might grab a coffee. Are we going for coffee?"

"I wouldn't be averse to it," Eimear said.

"Go, Lily," Sam said with a laugh. "We'll be fine, won't we, Jack?"

The baby had his fist in his mouth. Lily turned at the door and ran back to her husband and child, kissing them both goodbye. Sam whispered something to Lily, which resulted in a giggle and a blush from his wife. Maggie was envious of them. She'd love to have that kind of intimacy with someone.

They walked out of town, and Maggie and Lily put on their sunglasses. Eimear opted to squint.

"How are the wedding plans coming?" Lily asked Eimear.

Eimear groaned. "What a hassle. You know what I would like to do? I'd like to go to Las Vegas and get married by an Elvis impersonator."

"Then why don't you?" Maggie asked.

"I don't know. Don't want to disappoint people."

"It's your day. Do what you want," Maggie said.

Walkers, cyclists, and people pushing prams crowded the footpath along the cliffs. The day was bright, the Atlantic was calm, and sunlight glinted across the dark water, making it sparkle. It was a rare Irish sky: hardly a cloud in it.

Eimear asked, "What is it with all these people walking around with binoculars?" A flash of irritation passed across her face. Maggie didn't know if it was from the subject or the fact that the sun was in her eyes.

"Bird watchers," Lily said. "I don't know what's going on. They've been coming into the café all week. All I can say is they like coffee and baked goods!"

Maggie made note of all the people with binoculars. Eimear was right; there seemed to be a surplus of them.

"What are you going to do about your home?" Lily asked Maggie.

"What do bird watchers have to do with your home?" Eimear asked.

"Nothing. It's the recent development. The golf course and the resort," Maggie said.

"How is that going to affect your home?" Eimear asked.

"They're buying all the properties adjoining the McDougal farm," Lily explained.

"You're going to sell your cottage?" Eimear asked, frowning. "But you love that place."

"I don't want to sell, but I may be forced to," Maggie said.

"If you don't want to, then don't," Eimear said.

Maggie wished it were that straightforward.

"She may not have any choice in the matter," Lily said.

"Why?"

"I don't know the legalities of it, but they may force me to sell."

"That's not right!" Eimear said, her voice inching up an octave. She stopped walking right in the middle of the footpath. "What are you doing about it?"

"I'm not sure yet," Maggie said.

Eimear shook her head. "That's not good enough. Go see a solicitor straightaway. Don't dawdle."

Lily lifted one eyebrow.

"I will," Maggie promised. Eimear was right. It was time to see a solicitor and see what say she had in all of this. If any.

On Thursdays, April opened the shop, as Maggie taught her tai chi class in the morning. Maggie had planned to have a lie-in but woke early with the rising of the sun after a restless night. After a lingering walk on the beach with Rufus, Daisy, and Twinkle, she ate a hearty bowl of porridge and made herself a cup of rooibos tea.

Maggie sat down at the old wooden kitchen table with her cup of tea. She had some time before her class.

There were only two options that she could think of: either sell to the developer or take on the American company and fight to save her home. She pulled out a paper and pen and listed the pros and cons of each decision.

If she sold her home, she'd be able to take the cash and move anywhere. She could start over, start fresh. There could be a brand-new build. A house whose walls weren't eighteen inches thick or uneven. A floor that didn't slope so much that butter in the cast-iron skillet pooled to one side. Hot water on demand instead of having to turn on the immersion and wait for the water to heat. The things she'd be able to do or have. The list was endless.

Looking around, her eyes came to rest on the framed photo of her and her grandparents on her college graduation day. Nana and Granddad flanked her, their arms around her, beaming. A lump formed in her throat and her eyes stung. After all they'd done for her, how could she just up and sell the home they'd left her?

There was no way she could leave the home she'd grown to love. Everywhere she looked was a memory. Of her life there. Of her grandparents and all they had done for her after her parents died. She couldn't imagine living anywhere else. How could she?

She wondered if she would have any support from anyone in town. There'd be some, people like Olive who were concerned about the environment. There were those who wouldn't be too thrilled with the town being overrun with tourists. And there were bound to be a few people who'd object to it because they abhorred any change at all. But the prospect of jobs being dangled like a carrot was just too enticing for a lot of people. And Maggie would agree if things were different.

Eimear was right. She needed to contact a solicitor. She wrote that down on her list and starred it. If she had any rights, it would help to find out what they were.

Jake might not get planning permission right away, but that didn't mean Maggie should wait to find out the outcome. It would be better if she played offense rather than defense.

Maggie looked out the window and saw that the sky had turned gray, and she sighed.

And then there were of course the cons of the resort itself. Would flying golf balls ruin the walking trail that skirted along the cliffs? Hard to enjoy a leisurely stroll if you were dodging golf balls. And what about the resort itself? Granted, with tourists came extra cash, but would they overrun Ballygap? Would the quaint seaside town turn into a seedy place? And what about any bars or discos at the hotel?

A few townspeople came to mind and Maggie scribbled their names down on her list. Her next thing to do would be to contact them about forming a coalition to oppose the construction of this golf course and resort.

The thing she had on her side was that in Ireland, planning permission for corporate development was a notoriously slow process. It wasn't like she was going to be chucked out in the morning with all her belongings as they razed her house behind her. There was time. But it was best to be prepared so as not to be blindsided.

Jake Ballard must have already applied for planning permission because a meeting had been organized.

But Maggie wouldn't just sit around and wait to hear what the final decision was going to be. It was time to start voicing her objections.

After a while, she pushed it aside and moved her mind to other, more immediate things: namely her tai chi class that she needed to get to, and the organization meeting for the Ballygap 5k Fun Run, which was being held on Saturday at the parish hall.

———— *ele* ————

The parish hall in town was the perfect setting for Maggie's weekly tai chi class. She'd started the class two years previous, and it had become established among the community. Initially, there had been some resistance and her first class had only two participants. Not to be deterred, Maggie soldiered on, and now her class had grown to a respectable thirteen, including her Aunt Eileen.

Maggie wore a pair of black yoga pants and an oversized T-shirt that fell to her thighs. She had pulled her hair up into a loose, messy bun, and she'd removed her bangles from her wrist so as not to cause a distraction for her class.

Her class broke down into eleven women and two men. One of the men, Mel, a retired butcher, had come to her a year ago after having some balance problems. Once any neurological disease or disorder had been ruled out, his GP, Sam Rooney, had suggested Maggie's tai chi class.

"I see the Yank is here in town," Mel said. "They don't waste any time once they decide to do something."

"But it's going to create a lot of jobs for our area," Delia said. Maggie sympathized with her. Delia was a widow with teenaged children. She'd been unemployed for several years.

Maggie said, "Shall we get started?"

Once the group spread out in a line, Maggie led them through a series of warm-up exercises. She taught the Beijing twelve-step form of tai chi.

She had just led them through the movements of Part the Wild Horse's Mane and had begun White Crane Spreads its Wings when the door at the back of the parish hall opened and Jake entered.

Maggie sighed. Was he really going to bother her here?

When Maggie caught his eye, he smiled at her. She ignored that feeling of wanting to melt. "Can I help you?"

"I'm here for the tai chi class." He walked toward her like he owned the place. She gritted her teeth at his attitude. Who did he think he was?

"Unfortunately, we're halfway through our course. Besides," she added sweetly, "we like all negative energy left outside."

He laughed and when he did, his countenance relaxed. She liked the way his eyes crinkled up in the corners. She almost smiled in response. Almost.

He shrugged, a smile lingering on his face. He continued to approach, closing the distance between them.

Maggie took a step back and swallowed hard.

"The class is closed to outsiders, then?" he asked.

Maggie winced at the implication. She was aware that all the eyes of her group were traveling back and forth between her and him.

"No, of course not," she said, her voice going higher than she would have liked.

"Shall I stand anywhere then?" he asked, his eyes not leaving her face.

She wanted to tell him to go stand in the car park but bit her tongue. "Yeah, I don't care, find a spot," she said and turned her back to him, moving on with the class. It took a few steps before the entire class was back in sync. She hoped he didn't hold them up.

The last thing she wanted was the man that was trying to throw her out of her home to hijack her class. And yet, here he was. She sighed and took a deep breath.

He found a spot at the back of the class next to the widow, Delia. As Maggie faced the class, leading them through the moves, she noticed that every few minutes, he said something to Delia that elicited a laugh and smile from the widow. She'd never seen Delia so animated. The woman had had a rough life these past few years. Her husband died when her children were small, and it hadn't been easy. Eileen had paid for her tai chi classes, which was only known to the three of them. Maggie had to give Jake credit if he could make Delia laugh. But she was not about to call him Man of the Year.

From her point in the front of the room, she continued with the tai chi routine. Out of the corner of her eye, she kept watch over Jake. She expected to see him struggling; she expected to have to point out the correct form. She wanted to tell him he was doing it wrong. But either he was a natural or he'd done this before. At the end of the set, she commented on his proficiency.

"I studied under a master in Beijing," he explained.

Well, la-di-da, she thought. Some of the older women in the class regarded him with awe. She wanted to jump up and down and warn them not to fall for this charlatan. A wolf in sheep's clothing and all that.

Jake turned to Sheila, who stood nearest to him, and told her she had excellent form. Sheila, the local librarian, who was shy on the best of days, lit up at his compliment. *Don't fall for it*, Maggie wanted to yell. *Stay strong!*

As the session wound up, she reminded the group about the organizational meeting and sign-up for the Ballygap Fun Run on Saturday. As a parting shot, she announced, "I'll also have a sign-up form at the shop for anyone who opposes the McDougal farm being turned into a golf course." Jake grinned and her students nodded but said nothing.

Usually at the end of the class, her students lingered and chatted for a while. They were such a lovely group. But today, they were enthralled by the American and swarmed around him. Even Mel was engaging in conversation with him. Maggie stayed apart, packing her things up in her satchel and trying not to roll her eyes every time Jake said something that resulted in a twitter of laughter.

If he weren't trying to push her out of her home, she'd be enthralled, too. How could you not be?

Her aunt approached her, looked back at the rest of them, and lowered her voice. "Don't pay any mind to them, Maggie. Once the shine wears off, they'll lose interest. Trust me." She gave Maggie a reassuring smile. Eileen had always had her back, for as long as Maggie could remember. She couldn't help but smile herself.

Maggie waved goodbye to the group, told them she'd see them next week, and walked out with her aunt, stopping next to the older woman's car.

Her aunt placed her hand on Maggie's arm and looked at her. "How are you? How about lunch sometime next week?"

"I'm fine, really. And yes, I would love to go to lunch."

Maggie waited until her aunt was in her car and waved as she drove off. As she walked toward Slainte Mhaith, she heard Jake call out her name from behind.

"Maggie, wait up," he said.

Instead of stopping, she picked up her pace.

"Maggie!" he called, louder.

As people from the town were now starting to look at them, she stopped. Her shop was in her sights, but still, to prevent tongues from wagging, she stopped mid-step and let him catch up with her.

"Hey, I want to know how much I owe you for the classes," he said. He pulled his wallet from his back pocket.

She pursed her lips together, not missing how he had said "classes" in the plural. With a tight smile, she asked, "Will you be returning for more?"

He shrugged and smiled. "I'm here for the summer. I might as well." He put his hands on his hips and joked, "I might give you a few pointers."

"I might give you a few pointers as well," she snapped. Who did he think he was? The cheek of him!

He laughed, which she found infuriating. His cavalier attitude was beginning to stick in her craw.

"Other than my home, what else is it you want?"

He smiled again, raising an eyebrow. Maybe this worked on other women, but it wasn't going to work on her. No matter how handsome he was, she would not succumb to his charms. She didn't care how easy his manner was, reminding her of a summer's day. She would remain on guard. No matter how she felt when he looked at her, she would remain resolute and keep him at arm's length.

"Will you let me take you to dinner?" he asked.

In a parallel universe, she would have loved to go to dinner with him. And a part of her was secretly pleased that he wanted to take her out. But her posture stiffened and her muscles went rigid. "Whatever for? So you can wine and dine me out of my home?"

"Maybe I just want to get to know you better," he said.

"And then after you know me, kick me out of my home?" she cried.

"Come on, let's put our differences aside for one evening and go for dinner," he said.

"No, thank you." She turned to step away, and he called out after her. She faced him.

"Maggie, if I weren't building this golf course, would you go out with me?"

Maggie took a step backward and smiled. "You'll never know now, will you?"

She turned around and with her shop directly ahead, she picked up her pace.

When Maggie sailed through the front door of her shop, April stood at the counter, sipping licorice tea from a china cup.

"Was that the Yank I saw you talking with? He reminds me of a film star," she said.

"He's all flash and no substance," Maggie muttered as she headed back to her office.

Maggie closed the office door and thought, yes, if things had been different, she would have gone out to dinner with him. She wouldn't even have had to think about it.

CHAPTER TEN

J AKE'S PLAN FOR THE day was to meet up with homeowners whose properties abutted the McDougal farm. Although Greystone hadn't yet received planning permission, it
was best to be prepared for any future obstacles. He got in
touch with eight homeowners and set up six appointments.
There were two whom he hadn't been able to reach, but he
would keep trying. He didn't even bother contacting Maggie.
Not yet. But he was going to talk to her again.

His first appointment was with Peg O'Malley. He'd spoken
with Peg once already when she had approached him at the
town meeting. She was a woman who barely stood five feet tall,
but she'd come at him with a force that belied her short stature.
Almost giddy, she hadn't immediately introduced herself, just
smiled wide and asked, "Where do I sign?"

She'd been so enthused that Jake went against everything
he'd been taught and asked her if she'd like to consult her
attorney, but she'd cut him off and told him to bring the
paperwork by as soon as possible. Of course, there was no
paperwork drawn up as yet, not before the purchase of the

McDougal property was approved, but that hadn't dampened Peg's enthusiasm.

Peg O'Malley's house was an older bungalow on a rectangular piece of property that led straight back to the cliffs and the Atlantic Ocean below. Next to the main house lay the ruins of an older stone house and numerous outbuildings. Peg had told him it was no longer a working farm. He knew at a glance Greystone would bulldoze everything.

The bungalow was peach-colored with cream trim around the windows, and there were red flowers everywhere. He couldn't identify any of them aside from the roses and geraniums, but the overall feel was one of welcoming hospitality.

Before he even lifted his hand to ring the bell, the front door flew open and Peg stood there smiling, her blue eyes twinkling.

"Come in, come in," she said with a wave of her hand.

He followed her inside and down a narrow hallway to the kitchen at the back of the house. The entire place was wallpapered and carpeted and had a pleasant smell of vanilla. There was a large fern on a pedestal that he almost knocked over.

"Sorry about that, I need to do something about that plant," she said. "But it thrives in that corner for whatever reason. Every time I try to move it to another location in the house, it starts dying."

Peg invited him to sit down at the kitchen table. A long window overlooked the back garden, and beyond that, the Atlantic. But Peg seemed oblivious to it as she went about making two cups of tea. Jake wondered if one became impervious to it after a while. Maybe after a time, you became immune to its charms and didn't notice it at all.

Once the tea was made, Peg pulled up a chair next to him at the table. She was all smiles.

"Can we get right down to business?" she asked.

Jake laughed. "We can."

"I'll go first," she said.

Jake grinned. He liked this woman.

"I have no attachment to this place. It was my husband's home place. I want to move to Spain, but I want a good price for my land."

"You don't like it here?" he questioned, taking a sip of his tea. He drank it black, and it was pretty strong. "It's so beautiful," he said with a glance out the back window to the ocean.

"Come by in November or January," she scoffed. "It's very bleak."

He nodded.

"Come on, now," she said.

Jake had to laugh; it wasn't like he was going to hand her a pile of cash that afternoon. But he humored her and went through the process step by step of what would happen once they received planning permission.

"How much were you looking for in a buyout?" he asked.

"Well, nothing less than fair market value," she countered.

"Of course. I suggest you get an auctioneer out here to give you a valuation, and we'll use that as our starting point when we get clearance to make you an offer," he said.

"Will do," she said.

He finished his tea, thanked her for her time, and told her he'd be in touch.

At the door, he stopped mid-step and verbalized his thoughts. "If only everyone could be as agreeable as you, Peg."

Peg laughed. "Well, the Irish have a strong attachment to their land historically, but I think you mean Maggie Moran, don't you? It's more than that for Maggie."

"What do you mean?"

"When Maggie arrived here as a young girl, she was a mess. And who could blame the poor child? She'd just lost both of her parents. That first year was not only tough on her, but on the Morans as well. Maggie was skipping school and staying out late, but her grandparents persevered and after a year, Maggie settled down."

"I'll have to tread carefully," Jake said. He ran his thumb along his bottom lip, staring at the ground, lost in thought.

"Good luck with that. She'll never sell that house."

"We'll see."

"Like I said, good luck. You're going to need it," she said, as he stepped out onto the footpath.

ele

As Jake walked to his next meeting, he noticed a young man along the footpath that skirted the McDougal property. Despite his youthful appearance—he couldn't have been over thirty—he was dressed with no regard for style in cargo shorts, a T-shirt, and a cargo vest. Jake watched with curiosity as the man lifted his binoculars, peered through them, and dropped them, leaving them to hang around his neck as he scribbled in a notebook with intense concentration. He'd repeated this routine several times by the time Jake approached him.

Intrigued, Jake asked, "What are you looking at?"

The young man looked up at him, startled. "Just taking some notes on the wildlife."

Jake smiled and nodded, assuming he was there to do the environmental study commissioned by the county council. Not wanting to interrupt the man further, he said, "Well, I'll let you get back to it."

As he walked back to town, he glanced over his shoulder at the man and smiled. The man continued to use his binoculars and jot down more notes. He appeared thorough. It impressed Jake. The council didn't waste any time getting things done.

———*ele*———

Jake was becoming a regular around town, and people had begun waving and calling out to him by name when he passed them. Not only was that good for business, but Jake found he was enjoying becoming immersed in the community. And what better event to take part in than the annual Ballygap Fun Run? Particularly since it would give him a chance to interact with Maggie.

Jake set the flyer he'd picked up at the supermarket on the kitchen counter. Noah was up and dressed.

"Ballygap has an annual fun run, a 5k sort of thing," Jake opened. "What do you say?"

Noah snorted. "No, I don't think so."

"It might be fun if we did it together. Plus, it might be a good way to get to know people while we're here. There's a sign-up this afternoon," Jake said.

Noah shook his head. "I am not hanging out with my father all summer. How lame." He pulled on a light rain jacket as it had started to sprinkle outside.

Jake frowned. "Where are you going?"

"A bike ride with Roisin," Noah said, but his face reddened.

Jake watched after his son, hoping the camaraderie they had shared at Newgrange wasn't a one-time thing. He decided they'd do something together soon.

Once the breakfast dishes were loaded into the dishwasher, Jake left for the parish hall, where the sign-up was taking place.

He was looking forward to it. He loved running, especially when it was for a good cause.

As he approached the hall, people of all ages, both men and women, were streaming inside. He headed through the double doors alongside Olive, the octogenarian, whom he'd met at the town meeting. Since then, he seemed to run into her everywhere, and when he did, he'd always stop to talk. Despite her objection to the development, she'd been a good sport.

Her eyes widened, and she laughed. "You again! We have to stop meeting like this." She giggled like a schoolgirl and added, "People are going to talk."

"Let them talk! What do we care? Throw caution to the wind, Olive," he teased. This resulted in more giggles.

"Oh, you're too much," she said.

"We could sign up and run together," he suggested.

She snorted. "At my age, I'm lucky I can get upright. But thanks for thinking of me," she said, laughing. "And as much as I'd love to join you, I'll be manning the kitchen that day."

Jake nodded, held the door open for her, and followed her in.

The parish hall was packed. At the far end, above the stage, a banner announced "Ballygap's 8th Annual Fun Run." A number of volunteers with clipboards and sign-up sheets sat behind a long table running parallel to the stage.

Jake was surprised to see Noah arrive with Roisin. He lifted an eyebrow at his son and smirked. Noah gave him the stink eye, but otherwise ignored him.

Jake approached them. "Hello, Roisin."

Noah rolled his eyes.

"Hi."

Jake watched the way Noah kept looking sideways at the girl, with her bright red hair and green eyes. If he didn't know any better (but he did), he'd say his son was smitten. He smiled to himself.

"What brings you two here?" Jake asked.

"We're signing up for the race. We're going to cycle it, aren't we, Noah?" Roisin said, looking up at Noah.

"But I thought you said—" Jake started, about to recount their conversation earlier that morning.

Noah cut him off. "Never mind, Dad. Come on, Roisin, let's find the sign-up sheet."

"Bye, Jake," Roisin said as they walked away.

"Have fun," Jake called after them.

His day brightened even more when he spotted Maggie. She stood amid the throng, directing people to various sign-up sheets at the table. Jake watched her for a moment: the abundance of dark hair, the sharp blue eyes. She wore a gauzy dress that swished around her as she moved. He could have stared at her all day. When she spotted him, she scowled. Jake wondered how long the thaw would take. But then he realized that if he built his golf course and she lost her home, there'd never be a thaw.

Chapter Eleven

MAGGIE WAS SATISFIED WITH the turnout for the sign-up of the Ballygap Fun Run. The event would involve a five-kilometer course for runners and walkers, and a lengthier course for cyclists. Looking around the hall, she estimated there'd be more than enough volunteers and entrants. She crossed her fingers that the day would be a success. And hopefully, rain-free.

Tom Duffy was in charge of organizing volunteers who would stand along the route and direct the runners. There was another list for the pre-run setup. This involved placing signs that read "Race in progress" and spray-painting fluorescent orange arrows on the road in the direction of the race. Eimear was in charge of having stations of bottled water placed throughout the course. Olive oversaw a list of volunteers who would help her with kitchen duties and the post-race party. Lily was in charge of the list for snacks and treats, and Eileen had the longest line in front of her section of the table. This was the line for entrants to sign up and pay their fee.

Jake Ballard's appearance tempered Maggie's good mood. Would he show up at every local event? Become part of the Ballygap landscape like the rest of them? She hoped not. He appeared to be ingratiating himself to everyone in town. Maggie thought it was pathetic.

She remained focused on race day. After the race, everyone would come back to the hall and there would be a party of sorts, along with a raffle of prizes. All the monies collected from the race would go to local charities, with the main one being the Ballygap Clifftop Rescue. Swimmers and walkers got into all kinds of trouble, and the addition of a rescue unit fifteen years ago had been a game changer. Just last year, a rogue wave had swept a young man out to sea, but luckily, he had been rescued in time, averting a tragedy.

Jake stood next in line in front of Eileen, awaiting his turn. Deciding she should try her best to discourage him, Maggie approached him.

"Are you entering the race?" she asked.

"I am. I'm looking forward to it," he said.

"It's unnecessary for you to join," she said. Discouraging him without appearing to be rude would be tricky.

"Are you prohibiting me from partaking in the race?" he asked. He was grinning. She wished he wouldn't do that. Or be so nice. It would be a lot easier to dislike him if he were mean or dodgy.

They were interrupted by Eileen. "Mr. Ballard—"

"Please call me Jake."

"Jake, of course you can enter the race! Everyone is welcome and we're delighted to have you," Eileen said. She cast a pointed look at her niece.

Maggie looked at her aunt as if she had lost her mind. Whose side was she on? Just two days ago at the tai chi class, she'd seemed sympathetic. Eileen stood up from her chair, came around the table and said to Jake, "Just fill out that form, and I'll be right back." She moved over to Maggie.

"Can I talk to you for a minute?" Eileen said, pulling on Maggie's sleeve.

Maggie followed her aunt through the door that led to the empty kitchen.

"What are you doing?" Eileen demanded. "Do not be rude to Jake Ballard."

"I don't want him just coming in here and acting like he belongs," Maggie said.

"Don't be like that, Maggie. This town isn't like that, and you know that better than anyone else," Eileen said softly.

Maggie, chastised, felt her cheeks reddening.

"I know this is personal for you, but he is trying to do some good," Eileen said.

"What happened since Thursday?" Maggie asked, trying to keep the sharpness out of her tone.

"Tom told me this morning that Greystone made a substantial donation to the Ballygap Clifftop Rescue. It's all they're talking about down there. But Jake doesn't want anyone to know." Eileen raised her eyebrows and whispered, "Five figures."

There were no secrets in a small town in Ireland. Whether or not Jake wanted people to know was moot. It would somehow get out and if her aunt was telling her this bit of news, then it was already spreading through the community. Like wildfire. This upset Maggie. Could no one see through him?

"Can't you see he's trying to buy us?" Maggie hissed, disappointed that her aunt appeared to be another townsperson under his spell.

"Maybe he is!" Eileen said. "But I also know that his money is going to do a lot of good in Ballygap, and this town needs it."

"Even if it means trampling over people?" Maggie asked, her voice rising an octave.

Eileen sighed. "Not everyone is going to be happy about this development. But it's for the greater good of the town."

Maggie looked at her aunt in disbelief. She had gone over to the dark side. And it had only taken two days.

"But what about those of us who'll be most affected by it?" Maggie asked. "Don't we get a say?"

"Of course you do!" Eileen said. "But the minority should never dictate to the majority."

"And what about Nana and Granddad's house? Doesn't that mean anything to you?" Maggie fumed.

Something flared behind Eileen's eyes. "Don't be ridiculous."

Her aunt stomped off and Maggie sighed. She did not want to be fighting with her aunt. She laid the blame at the feet of Jake Ballard.

Jake held court at the end of the table. Maggie avoided that area. People surrounded him, and she couldn't help but notice they were all women, including April. *Oh no, not you, too.*

Maggie leaned over to see how many people had signed up on Olive's list.

Beside her, Olive mused, "He's so charming. It would be hard to say no to him." She appeared thoughtful. "If I were a lot younger, I'd let him park his shoes under my bed." She sighed.

Maggie looked at her in alarm. "Stay with me, Olive. We're trying to save the coastline, remember?"

Olive snapped out of it. "Oh, right." She giggled. "It's hard not to like him. He's so handsome."

"That's what he's counting on!" Maggie cried. Was she the only one that was able to see it?

Maggie looked at Jake across the hall and narrowed her eyes. Just the other day, she'd caught him carrying Peg O'Malley's groceries to her car. The older women wished they had a son like him, although—she glanced at Olive—in some cases there was nothing maternal about it. Girls in their twenties giggled when he saluted them on the street. How could they all be so blind?

There was no way she'd be succumbing to his charms. He used his charm to his advantage, that was for certain. It made Maggie angry how he just rolled into Ballygap and expected everyone to fall at his feet.

While she was helping to set up the tables of sandwiches and cakes, Jake appeared at her side. She ignored the intoxicating smell of his aftershave. She ignored how the fine hairs on her arms stood up when he was near her. Or at least, she tried to. *This cannot be happening*, she thought. *I cannot find the enemy attractive.* She needed to broaden her horizons a bit, maybe join some clubs with both male and female members. Or maybe join an online dating app.

"Can I help with anything?" Jake asked.

Maggie straightened up and smirked. "I think I can handle it."

"Are you sure? I could help carry out the platters," he tried again.

He was pathetic.

"Look, Mr. Ballard—"

Jake interrupted her. "I hadn't realized we were on such formal terms."

"We are," Maggie said. Under no circumstance was he to harbor the delusion that they were on familiar terms. Or even courteous ones. She glanced over at the gaggle of women on the other side of the room who were standing there, looking over at Jake. "You may have charmed the pants off of them, but I can assure you, you won't do the same to me."

"But you're not wearing pants," he deadpanned.

Maggie ignored him and nodded toward the group of admirers. "You see what I mean."

Jake glanced in their direction and smiled and nodded in acknowledgment. "I must try harder, as they all still seem to be wearing their pants." He had put his hands on his hips, and it was hard to miss the way his biceps stretched the sleeves of his shirt. Maggie gave a little cough and forced herself to look away.

"Ugh," she huffed and walked away, his laughter ringing in her ears.

———*ℓℓ*———

Maggie was still fuming about Jake while she stocked jars of lavender honey at her shop on Monday morning. As she placed the new stock behind the old jars, her thoughts seemed to be stuck in a loop: She wasn't selling her home. Period. Why should she be forced to move just because someone wanted to swing a golf club around?

With her posture rigid and her lips pinched, she lifted the last jar out of the box. It slipped from her grasp and crashed to the floor, the glass breaking. The honey, thick and golden, flowed onto the floor.

April appeared at her side, guiding Maggie out of the aisle. "Go for a walk, take some deep breaths, and I'll clean this up," she instructed.

Maggie nodded, her lips stretched into a thin line.

April closed the door behind her, and Maggie stood outside for a minute, trying to regulate her breathing. She drew in a deep breath, focusing on her inhalations and exhalations until the threat of tears dissolved. The air was chilly, and she'd left her poncho back in her office at the back of the store. It wasn't worth returning; she was going to follow April's advice. Although April had her faults, the thing she loved more than anything was taking care of people. Maggie was trying to steer her toward nursing or some form of homeopathic medicine, but April would just shrug, holding her teacup, and say, "I'm happy here. I help people here."

Maggie started walking and found herself in the center of town. She looked around, paying particular attention to the closed-down businesses and boarded-up shops. It seemed as if every year, another business closed its door for the last time. Just last year, it had been Keely's, a little shop that carried all sorts of household goods, from bedsheets to plungers. She used to accompany her nan there on the odd occasion. But Mr. Keely, who had operated the business for almost sixty years, had died, and his children had no interest in continuing. It had been an enormous loss to the town.

She passed people on the footpath, nodding or smiling at them in acknowledgment. One even called out, "Great news about the golf course, isn't it?"

"Oh, it sure is," Maggie replied. She spotted the two-storey building of her solicitors, Gentilhomme, White & Sons, and darted across the street. Eimear was right; it was time to seek legal advice.

Dan Gentilhomme was born of an Irish mother and a French father. He had been her grandparents' solicitor when they were alive, and she'd gone to him herself when she opened her business and also when she'd drawn up a will. He was getting on in years, but still active.

Mary Masterson manned the reception desk in the front of the office.

"Is Dan in, Mary?" Maggie asked. Mary, a neighbor of Eileen's, had been with the firm for as long as it had been operating.

"He is," Mary answered. "How are you?"

Maggie nodded. She knew there'd be no seeing the solicitor until pleasantries and news passed between them.

"I'm fine. The shop is fine. April is fine."

Mary gave a slow nod, satisfied. She stood up from her chair, her back ramrod straight, and said, "Let me see if he can see you now."

"Thanks, Mary," Maggie said.

Mary soon returned. "Go on back, Maggie."

Maggie nodded her thanks and headed to the back of the building, where Dan had his office.

The older man stood up from his desk when Maggie knocked and entered.

"Maggie! This is a pleasant surprise!"

Maggie smiled and nodded.

"Sit down, sit down," he said. "Can I get you a cup of tea?"

She shook her head and sat in the chair opposite his desk, smoothing her dress beneath her.

The solicitor was showing his age. His gray hair matched his pallor, and he looked shrunken in his suit. His office was crowded with furniture, and there were stacks of files on every available space: tabletops, his desk, and the floor. There had to

be decades worth of papers, with a single clear path from the
door to the front of the desk and around it. Maggie worried
about him tripping over all these obstacles. Especially at his
age.

"I'm here because of my home," Maggie started, not wanting
to hold him up.

Dan sighed. "And the American developer who will most
likely want to buy it off you."

"Exactly," Maggie said. "Am I in danger of losing my home
to this developer, even if I don't want to sell?"

Dan hesitated. Maggie's heart sank. She'd expected Dan to
reassure her.

He leaned back in his chair and steepled his fingers together.
"It depends on how badly they want your property. Could we
prove they could still build their golf course without acquiring
your land?"

"Can we prove that?" Maggie countered.

Dan shrugged.

"What legal ground are they standing on?" she asked.

"There is something called a compulsory purchase order,
where the government can take your property, with compensation of course, but without your consent," he explained.

"But that's the government," she said. She understood how
that might apply for public works like roads and other infra-
structure, but a golf course? That couldn't be slotted into that
column, could it?

Dan tried to reassure her. "Maggie, this is only in the de-
velopmental phase. Many things can go wrong: companies go
bankrupt, economies go into recession, etcetera. Try not to
worry about it."

"Easier said than done."

"Right now, your best bet is to lodge an appeal with An Bord Pleanála. If the developer obtains planning permission, lodge your objection. You would only have four weeks, so don't waste any time. If you lose that appeal and An Bord Pleanála approves the project, you could take it to court." He paused. "But I warn you, Maggie, that could be very costly. And if you lose, you might be liable for the developer's court costs as well." He studied her for a moment and asked, "Is it worth financial ruin?"

Maggie swallowed hard. Her home was worth everything to her.

Dan turned the conversation to general pleasantries, and Maggie tried to stay engaged but couldn't. Her mind raced and wandered.

She stood up. "I've taken up enough of your time, Dan." She thanked him, shook his hand, and left, more disheartened than before.

CHAPTER TWELVE

D URING HIS CALL TO California, Jake informed his father of Maggie being a possible holdout. He softened the blow with the word "possible."

"Apply some pressure to get her to sell," Don Ballard said.

"Her home is three hundred years old," Jake replied.

"Whose side are you on?"

Jake didn't know why he was defending her.

"That alone is good reason to buy her out," his father said. "You know that saying, 'They don't make them like they used to'? Well, I say thank goodness!"

"Dad, I will not intimidate people," Jake said. And he wouldn't.

"Don't go soft, son, this is business."

"Will you let me handle it?"

"I'm letting you handle it," Don said.

Once the business side of things was concluded, Jake said, "Noah tells me you're thinking of taking him to France next year."

"Yes. He's been emailing the two of us." Don laughed. "And let me tell you, Noah is a bright and funny kid. His emails are the highlight of our day."

"So, France," Jake said again.

"Yes, your mother is looking into it. That's if you and Nadine are on board," his father said.

"I'll talk to Nadine, but I don't think it will be a problem," Jake said. Nadine had always gotten on well with his parents, especially his mother.

"It'll be an enjoyable trip for the three of us."

"I'm glad. It sounds like fun," Jake said. He was surprised at this development between Noah and his parents. And he was all for it.

"And he has himself a girlfriend! This Roisin sounds lovely," his father said.

"He's told you about Roisin?" Jake asked, a little taken aback.

"Sure, he asked your mother and me for some advice back when he first met the girl."

"He did?" Jake asked. "What did he want to know?"

"Oh, I can't tell you that," his father said, with a hint of annoyance. "That would betray a confidence."

Jake rolled his eyes. It hurt a bit that his son went to his grandparents for advice and didn't come to him. Especially since they were living in the same house for three months.

"Anyway, he's a great kid and your mother and I are looking forward to seeing him when he returns to the States. We told him that if he wanted to come back early, he could spend part of his summer with us. But I don't think he wants to leave Roisin." His father added, laughing, "Ah, young love."

Jake got in an early morning run, then peeked in at Noah, who was sound asleep. After his shower and shave, he decided he had time to see Maggie.

As Maggie's cottage by the sea came into view, Jake's thoughts drifted toward her. He felt like a teenager with a serious crush. As he walked toward her house, his heart raced, making him feel jittery. Even if he was the last person she wanted to see. *A glutton for punishment, that's what I am*, he thought wryly as he walked toward her house.

All was quiet. The Dutch door was closed, and he hoped, locked. Her bike was gone. She must be at her shop.

Jake looked around the site, his hands on his hips, taking in the sprawling view of the Atlantic in one direction and the town in the distance in the other. The view alone would be reason enough for anyone to want to stay.

He headed to town and her shop. Maggie couldn't avoid him forever. But what did it say about him that he kept going back to her, even though she'd made her feelings about him and his development clear?

April sat on a high stool behind the counter, crocheting a purple and orange granny square. She wore ripped jeans and a T-shirt bearing the graphic of a cow above the words "Friends, not food." As soon as he entered, she set down her crocheting.

"Hello again," she said.

"Hi." Jake looked around the shop. "Is Maggie here?"

"She's in her office," April said. "Is there something I can help you with?"

"No, I'd like to speak to Maggie," he said.

"Her office is back here," April said, slipping out from behind the counter and heading toward the back of the shop. Jake followed her, breathing in the smell of incense and other fragrances he couldn't name. Did all health food shops smell the same? His eyes scanned the shelves, which displayed all sorts of vitamins and minerals, fresh herbs, a variety of different teas and coffees, all-natural cleaning products . . . nothing brand name or generic here. Every bit of shelving in the small space was put to good use.

Maggie sat at her desk, a candle burning in front of her.

April frowned. "Why are you burning a tranquility candle? What's wrong?"

Spotting Jake over April's shoulder, Maggie said, "Nothing's wrong. Just thought I'd try something different."

"Jake Ballard is here to see you."

"Yes?" Maggie enquired, looking at Jake. She didn't offer him a chair, but April came to the rescue.

"Why don't you sit in that chair there?" April suggested, indicating the only extra chair in Maggie's office, but Maggie waved her suggestion away.

"No, that's unnecessary. Mr. Ballard isn't staying," Maggie said.

April looked confused, which Jake suspected was a recurring look for Maggie's assistant.

"Oh," she said, and she lingered.

"That'll be all, April," Maggie said. "We don't want to hold Mr. Ballard up."

Jake tried not to cringe when she referred to him as "Mr. Ballard." It made him sound old. Or at least older. Older than her. Which he was.

Once April left, Jake leaned against the doorframe, kind of amused that she wouldn't invite him into the sanctuary of her office. He took no offense at this. It wasn't the first time he'd angered someone because of his business.

"I was hoping to sit down and talk with you," he said, starting the conversation.

"What for?" she asked.

Jake tilted his head and smiled. "I think you know why, Maggie."

"It's Miss Moran to you," she said.

"Your property is one of the ones I need to purchase for the resort to go ahead."

Her chin lifted and her blue eyes blazed. "It's not for sale."

Jake sighed. No matter where he went in the world or what property he developed, there was always going to be someone who was difficult. Someone who played hardball with him. Or tried to. Another part of his job was diplomacy: finding an agreeable solution for both Greystone and any holdouts. In the past, it usually involved offering more money. But somehow, Jake didn't think that would work with Maggie. He had to admit to respecting her for that.

He did not miss the storm that brewed behind those eyes.

"I'd like a chance to show you what a great opportunity this could be for you."

Maggie jumped up from her desk, pressing her clenched fists on the top of it. "Who are you to come into Ballygap and tell me I have to start my life over somewhere else? I am not starting my life over anywhere else. I'm staying put. By all means, build your golf course, but leave me out of it—"

"Oh, am I interrupting?" asked a voice from behind Jake. It was Olive.

"Are you stalking me, Olive?" Jake teased.

Olive stammered, then realized he was joking and slapped him playfully on the arm. "Oh, you're a joker, Jake."

Maggie stepped out from behind her desk, her gauzy dress clinging to her curves. "Olive, what can I do for you? Mr. Ballard was just leaving."

"I'm having a hard time sleeping." The old woman looked at Jake and winked. "All these recent developments have me up all night."

"Well, I'll leave you to it," Jake said with a smile to the old woman. He looked at Maggie, but she scowled at him.

He'd have to figure out a novel approach for her. She would not make things easy for him, that was for sure. But how to get her to come around? If there was one thing Jake relished, it was a challenge.

CHAPTER THIRTEEN

MAGGIE WATCHED JAKE LEAVE, feeling flustered. Shoving him as far as possible from her mind, she turned to Olive. "You said you were having trouble sleeping?"

One of the many things Maggie liked about Olive was that she was always open to trying new things. And she would report back if Maggie's recommendation worked.

"Yes, I don't know why." Olive sighed. "I mean, for all that is holy, to develop insomnia at my age!"

Maggie laughed but then asked, "Anything bothering you? Are you worrying about anything?"

Olive shook her head. "You know me, Maggie, I let the Lord do the worrying. That's his job. I've got enough to do."

Maggie knew this to be true. Olive was involved in just about everything in Ballygap, from the Tidy Towns Committee to the Flower Club to organizing bus trips to the shrine at Knock.

"I think I might have something for you," Maggie said, opening a drawer in her desk. She pulled out a small spray bottle and handed it to Olive.

"It's lavender oil. I make it myself," Maggie said. "Just spray a bit on your pillow at night. It's very relaxing."

"I love the smell of lavender," Olive enthused, turning the bottle around in her gnarled hand.

"Try this first and if it doesn't work, come back to me," Maggie said.

Olive pressed the pump and a light, lavender-scented mist filled the space between them. "Oh, that is lovely. How much do I owe you for this, Maggie?"

Maggie shook her head. "Nothing, I make the stuff myself with the lavender I grow."

Olive frowned. "You should charge for this."

Maggie laughed.

"Never mind," Olive said. "I can see it's going to be no use talking to you."

Maggie walked her out, and Olive paused and looked around the interior of the shop. "While I'm here, I should get some more turmeric."

Once Olive left, Maggie's thoughts drifted back to Jake and his reason for being in Ballygap. Blowing out a deep breath, she collapsed in her chair, trying not to let every meeting with Jake Ballard unnerve her. So far, it was failing.

She could easily dislike him for wanting her home. That alone should make her hate him. But Jake Ballard had a lot of attractive qualities that made it difficult for her to dislike him. Aside from being handsome, he was also funny, and he was kind. She'd seen how he talked to everyone he met. It seemed he always had time for people. He seemed genuine. It had been a long time since she'd had her head turned by anyone. She appreciated the male form in all its glory, but she rarely became so unsettled by it. Never had she found a man attractive who was trying to take something from her. That'd be enough to unsettle anyone.

Sighing, she swiped some loose strands of hair away from her forehead and tried to get recalibrated. It was best to focus on the reasons she didn't like him.

But instead she wondered what it would feel like to be held in his arms. To wrap her arms around him and pull him close and breathe in his aftershave. How would it feel to hear him whisper in her ear, his breath warm on her neck? The thought made her want to close her eyes and sigh.

She leaned forward and buried her face in her hands. How could she have a crush on this man?

It had been a long time since she'd had a crush on anyone. There had been that German tourist last year, the cyclist. With the encouragement of her friends, she'd summoned the courage, right before he left, to tell him how she felt, hoping for a long-distance relationship or at least someone to email, text, or write letters to. She'd been confident that he felt the same way she did. Had to. Must have.

He didn't. He hadn't. The German man had seemed surprised and had not hid it, and she had wanted to tuck her tail between her legs and run home. From that time, she'd become much more guarded around men. And needed to be more so with Jake Ballard. There was no way around it; they were fighting on opposite sides of a major battle.

She would keep reminding herself of this. Hopefully, if she told herself this over and over, it would not only diminish his place front and center in her mind, but also dampen the longing she felt for him.

Disheartened, Maggie left her office and headed to the front of the shop. She hoped April would distract her with some conversation. April did not disappoint. Her assistant was all up in arms over a large portion of the polar shelf splitting off and dropping into the ocean. Grateful for the distraction, Maggie put her arm around the girl and tried to comfort her.

"April, I know you're upset. But you should be proud of yourself. You're doing everything you can to save the environment," Maggie said. "You put your own contemporaries to shame."

April's eyes were full of tears that threatened to spill over. But she managed a nod, and Maggie gave her shoulder a squeeze. Maggie handed April a tissue to wipe her eyes.

The door opened, and a young man crossed the threshold. He was unfamiliar to Maggie.

The stranger looked to be in his late twenties and was wearing a khaki hat and a khaki vest with pockets over a T-shirt and cargo shorts. His ensemble was completed with thick wool socks, hiking boots, and a pair of binoculars hanging around his neck. He had a short mop of curly brown hair and he wore wire-rimmed glasses.

"Well, hello, stranger," April said, dabbing her eyes and quickly recovering from her lament over the arctic shelf.

Maggie rolled her eyes.

"Oh, uh, hi," he said, looking around, his eyes coming to rest on the coffee menu behind the counter.

Maggie gave him a minute and asked, "What can we do for you?"

"I'd like a takeaway coffee." He glanced back up at the menu. "Cappuccino, please."

"I'll get it," April said and went to make the coffee. Maggie had never seen April move so fast.

"What brings you to Ballygap?" Maggie asked.

The man lit up and exclaimed, "A corncrake!"

"Excuse me?" Maggie tilted her head as April giggled behind her.

The man grinned. "Oh, sorry. The corncrake. It's a bird. I'm from the Irish Bird Watcher Society. My name is Nigel Hayes." He shook Maggie's hand and then he reached across the counter and shook April's.

"Let go of his hand, April," Maggie whispered.

April reluctantly did so, and Nigel pushed his glasses up on his nose and blushed.

Oh boy, Maggie thought.

Nigel dragged his gaze away from April and looked at Maggie. "Someone emailed us with a photo of a bird they'd never seen before. I came down to look. I haven't seen it for myself yet, but I'll be here a few days to look for it. We're hopeful, of course."

"Where was it spotted?" Maggie repeated.

"Along the cliffs."

"Do you have a picture?" April asked, sliding his coffee across the counter. "Just so we can keep an eye out as well."

Nigel pulled his phone out of one of his many pockets and swiped the screen a few times. April came out from behind the counter, and she and Maggie leaned over the phone. Nigel had pulled up a photo showing a bird with a gray chest and chestnut-colored wings. Its head had bluish-gray cheeks and a short bill. Although Maggie enjoyed birds, especially as they heralded the arrival of spring, she wasn't that familiar with the various species.

"Is it a rare bird?" April asked.

"It used to be abundant here in County Clare, but no more. It's threatened with global extinction."

April's eyes widened.

"Do you think there's more than one?" Maggie asked.

Nigel smiled. "We're hopeful. I'm heading back down to see if I can spot it," he said, stealing a glance at April.

"Would you like some company?" April asked, smiling.

"I'd love some," Nigel said.

Maggie, doing something she'd never done before—play Cupid—said, "You know what, April? I think we're all caught up here if you wanted to take the rest of the day off."

April nodded. "Yeah, Mag, I think I will."

April headed out with Nigel, the two of them grinning at each other. Maggie smiled. Too bad attraction couldn't always be easy like that.

CHAPTER FOURTEEN

As Jake neared his home, he noticed Noah outside, standing at the stone wall that separated their house from the one next door. On the other side of the wall stood Roisin.

Well, this is interesting, Jake thought. He couldn't hear their conversation, but Noah had said something that resulted in a giggle from the girl.

As he walked toward the front door, he acknowledged them with a nod of his head, not wanting to interrupt. Noah rolled his eyes, and the girl laughed again.

Jake figured he'd just continue to play the uncool parent and said nothing but headed into the house and out of sight.

It was twenty minutes before Noah entered the house. The water for the spaghetti had just started to boil. Jake added some salt and then the pasta and gave it a stir.

"You seem to be seeing a lot of that Roisin," Jake said. He preheated the oven for the garlic bread and emptied a jar of sauce into a pot.

Noah shrugged. "Just someone to hang out with." Then, after a moment, he added, "She's nice."

Jake covered a baking tray with aluminum foil and removed a loaf of garlic bread from the freezer. "Just be careful, you know?"

"Dad!" Noah huffed.

"Yeah," Jake said. These conversations were never easy. But he'd been seventeen once, and he remembered it all too well.

"Do you have to ruin everything?"

Noah stomped out of the room and Jake called after him, "Dinner in fifteen minutes!"

"Whatever!" Noah shouted.

That went well. Maggie came to mind and Jake thought, *I really have a way with people.*

ele

Jake waited three days before he went to see Maggie again. He walked past Slainte Mhaith to make sure it was closed before he headed down the natural slope of the road toward the ocean, the beach, and Maggie's cottage.

The sun had begun its descent on the horizon and Jake could see lights on in the little cottage. There were a few walkers out on the path. Some nodded to him, some did not.

Faint music drifted out of an open window of the cottage. An interior light cast a golden glow on the garden as dusk fell.

Clearing his throat, he knocked on the door. There was the immediate response of barking dogs, making Jake laugh. The music stopped, and the top half of the door opened. Maggie stood there, framed in the doorway, appearing like a painting. Jake's mind went blank for a moment.

"Yes?" she asked.

"I was hoping we could talk—" he started.

Maggie shook her head before he even got the sentence out of his mouth. "That would be futile. You want my home, and I don't want to sell it. What's the point?" Behind her, one dog whined while the other barked. She shifted her knee and said over her shoulder, "Go on, Rufus, go."

She was tough. "Would you just hear my proposal?" he asked.

"The part where money is no object, and I can name my price?" she asked. She looked at him pointedly.

Jake's expression became pinched. She had an answer for everything. He remained undaunted.

"Look, there are some things that have no price tag attached," Maggie said. "In the corporate world, sentiment is disposable if it even exists at all."

"And you're basing this on . . .?" he asked, trying to conceal his irritation. Like most people, he didn't like to be judged.

Maggie smirked and lifted her chin. "Am I wrong?"

He didn't answer her question but said, "I can understand your not wanting to sell, as this is an impressive site." He waved his hand around toward the cliffs and the ocean. "But maybe there are other options for you."

"Such as?"

"Greystone could build you another cottage somewhere else, an exact replica of this one."

"And would it come with manufactured memories instead of the real ones I have with my home?"

He sighed. She certainly didn't make things easy. And yet he had to admit that her fierce determination was one of the many things he found attractive about her.

Jake remained silent.

"Good night, Jake," she said as she closed the door.

Jake sighed and moved on. He was going about this all wrong.

—— *ell* ——

Over the weekend, Jake made some plans for him and Noah. He'd ordered a hamper of food, which he collected early Saturday morning. The difficult part was rousing Noah from his blatant disinterest.

"Come on, it'll only take a few hours," Jake said. Noah was pumping air into the tire of his bike. "We'll climb that hill, look at some castle ruins and take some pictures. You can send them to your mother and your grandparents."

"I already made plans with Roisin," Noah protested.

"Just delay them," Jake said. "Tell her you'll be back by mid-afternoon." When Noah didn't respond, he added, "Come on, humor your old man."

"Fine!"

During the week, Jake had driven out and spoken to the farmer who owned the land. The man had been gracious and told him to come by Saturday morning after milking. Jake had asked what time that was and when the farmer had said eight, Jake wanted to laugh. There'd be no way Noah would be awake at that time, so he told him they'd be out around noon.

When he and Noah arrived at the farm, the farmer was just pulling in on his tractor. He jumped down and waved to them as he approached them. He was a short, wiry man wearing a flat cap and wellies.

"I'll show you the path, and I'd advise you to stay on it as I've got a bull in one of the fields and you don't want to mess with him," he warned.

Jake and Noah looked at each other, eyebrows raised.

"Also, the door to the tower is padlocked. I had some trouble a few years ago with trespassers who did some damage," the farmer said, shaking his head. He took a key off a ring and handed it to Jake. "Just bring it back to me when you leave. If you can't find me, you can drop it off at the house." He nodded toward the two-storey farmhouse.

"Will do," Jake said, pocketing the key.

Jake had taken the contents of the picnic hamper and distributed them between two backpacks, which they now carried. They set off on the path with Jake leading and Noah bringing up the rear.

The day was sunny. The sky was full of white, fluffy clouds, reminding Jake of a Paul Henry painting. The narrow path of gravel and stones was flanked on the left side by a compact blackthorn hedge. When the two of them arrived at the base of the hill, the path ended, but you could see a man-made trail that wound up the side of the hill.

The hill was steeper than Jake had imagined, and it took almost an hour to climb it. Not so much because of the height, but because of the rocky, uneven terrain. They talked little, each of them concentrating on their footing. Halfway up the hill, Jake found himself breathless.

"Dad, do you want to stop and rest?" Noah asked from behind.

"No, I'm fine," Jake said, looking up the hill, trying to gauge the distance. "There's not much farther to go."

"Well, slow down, there's no rush," Noah said.

Jake smiled to himself, wondering who the parent was.

When they reached the top, they were rewarded for their efforts. The ruin of a square, six-storey limestone tower stood in front of them—although the word "ruin" hardly seemed apt, as it was in pretty good shape for being almost six hundred years old. The remaining castle walls had been reduced over time until just the foundation remained.

The view was amazing. To the west, they looked toward Ballygap and beyond that, the Atlantic. The town was tucked between the sea and the farmland that lay to its north, south, and east. Jake spotted the extensive holding of the McDougal farm but could not see Maggie's cottage.

"This is so cool," Noah said, looking around.

"Come on, let's look inside," Jake said. He pulled the key from his pocket and unlocked the door.

There were six floors and a winding stone staircase. The interior was dark and empty, except for some litter and a dead crow on the floor. The embrasures allowed small slits of light to filter through, enough for them to see their way around. They took the worn steps to the top, investigating each floor. Each level looked like the one below. On the roof they found the remains of stilts, which would have been used by archers. They walked the perimeter of the roof, taking in the views. Noah took some photos with his phone, including a selfie of him and Jake.

"We should eat our lunch right here," Jake suggested. The top of the tower with its magnificent views made it the perfect spot.

"Good idea."

They settled on a place and pulled out their lunches from their backpacks.

"I don't know how you can eat that stuff cold," Jake said, nodding toward Noah's container of Moroccan chickpea tagine.

"It's good hot or cold," Noah said. He held out the container to Jake. "Here, try some."

Jake took a spoonful. It had a bit of a kick, but it was flavor-ful. "It's good."

"You sound surprised," Noah said with a laugh.

"Can I ask why you became a vegan?" Jake asked.

Noah shrugged. "Obviously, it's about the animals. I care about them." It seemed to be the opening Noah needed. He told his father about the cruelty inflicted on animals. He was quite intense about it. Not for the first time, Jake thought he and Nadine must have done something right to have raised such a caring individual. He asked Noah questions, wanting to learn more about his son. It was amazing to Jake how a child could be so different from his parents.

Before the divorce, Noah had had a goldfish, a canary, and a hamster. Now at Nadine's house, he had a dog and two cats. Jake had no pets as he traveled too much. The talk of animals reminded him of Maggie and her own menagerie.

Maybe he needed to be asking more questions of Maggie. Maybe it was time to investigate her why. Or maybe it was just time to listen.

CHAPTER FIFTEEN

M AGGIE WAS WORKING THE shop alone when Noah walked in with Roisin O'Connor. April had requested the day off to help Nigel track the bird and find a nest. April might not be the most motivated employee, but she was dependable. She rarely asked for time off and she never called in sick. Since she'd met Nigel, they'd been spending every moment together. In fact, Nigel didn't seem to be in any hurry to return home, wherever that was, and Maggie wondered how much that had to do with the quest to find this bird.

"Hi, Maggie," Roisin said.

"Hello, Roisin, hello, Noah," Maggie greeted them.

Noah rewarded her with a shy smile and a wave. Maggie saw how he stole glances at Roisin. It was a wonderful thing to be so young and so full of hope.

"How's your mother?" Maggie asked, turning her attention back to Roisin.

"She's well. She sent me down for some no-waste lavender soap, and she said I was to ask if you had any seaweed pesto," Roisin said.

"Not this week, but I'll have some next week," Maggie said. "I'll drop some off."

Roisin nodded, her gold hoop earrings swaying with the movement of her head. "Okay, I'll tell her."

"Seaweed pesto?" Noah wondered out loud, looking between Roisin and Maggie.

"It's so good," Roisin said. "On a cracker or some brown bread."

"I'll have to try it," Noah said.

"Would you like a jar as well?" Maggie asked.

"Sure, if it's not too much trouble," Noah said.

"It's no trouble at all." Maggie knew the Ballards lived next door to the O'Connors.

"I'll get the soap and wrap it up. Did you want coffee, Roisin?" Maggie asked.

"Yeah, I think I will. A soy latte," Roisin said.

Maggie nodded and said to Noah, "What about you? Would you like a coffee?"

He shrugged. "I'd like a chai latte."

Maggie got the bars of soap off the shelf, rang them up, and placed them in a plain brown paper bag. As they browsed through the shop, she made their drinks. The addition of the coffee machine to the shop had been a great idea. It was a big, complicated affair that had cost thousands of dollars, and she'd taken out a loan to finance it. But it had already paid for itself as people came in for the coffee, then ending up browsing and buying.

Roisin was chatting away, and Noah followed her around as they picked things off the shelf, looked at them, and put them back.

"Your drinks are ready. Can I get you anything else?" Maggie asked.

Noah sipped his latte. "I wish they made a tea bag that tasted like chai latte."

"Have you tried chai tea?" Maggie asked.

Noah nodded. "I have, but it's just not the same."

"Hold on," Maggie said. She slipped out from behind the counter and headed over to the shelves where the tea bags were kept. She pulled down two boxes and carried them back to the counter.

"This is the closest I've come after some experimenting," she said to Noah, holding up the two different boxes of tea. "Use one bag of chai tea and one bag of the Bengal Spice. I don't think you'll be disappointed. And you'll get two cups out of it."

"Thanks, Maggie, I'll give these a try," he said, smiling.

Roisin paid cash for her order, insisting on treating Noah. The teenage boy looked mortified but mumbled a thank-you. They walked out of the shop, carrying their beverages and their small brown bags. The last thing Maggie heard Roisin say was, "Will we walk onto the cliffs?"

Maggie smiled and watched as Noah stared at the redheaded girl, enthralled.

———ele———

The day before the race, Maggie took her aunt out to lunch. Once a month, they went out for a meal, and they always chose a restaurant outside Ballygap. Maggie looked forward to these outings, if only to get away for a bit and have a change of scenery.

They ended up about thirty kilometers from Ballygap, in a small village on the Clare-Galway border. They chose an old Irish pub with low ceilings, dark interior, and traditional Irish

music. Maggie loved these kinds of places. After a quick scan of
the menu, she opted for a bowl of carrot-and-parsnip soup and
a toasted ham-and-cheese sandwich. Her aunt ordered rocket
salad with greens and a bowl of soup. Maggie would wait to see
if there was room for dessert later.

"Have you lodged your objection with An Bord Pleanála?"
Eileen asked, picking up the water pitcher and filling their
glasses.

Maggie shook her head. "Not yet. I'm waiting to see if Jake
gets planning permission or not. But I've drafted my letter, so
it's ready to go." Maggie rattled off the objections she'd listed
in her letter.

"Good." Eileen regarded her niece for a moment.

"What?" Maggie asked. "Do I have something on my face?"

"No. You're very passionate about saving your home,"
Eileen said, eyeing her. "I can't help but wonder if it's the only
thing you're passionate about."

Aware that her aunt was staring at her, Maggie asked, "What
do you mean?"

"Don't be coy! I think you might have a crush on Jake Ballard." Eileen cut up her salad and chewed thoughtfully.

"I don't know what you're talking about," Maggie stammered. Her heart banged against the inside of her chest.

"I think you do. It's ironic, isn't it?"

"I cannot see the irony myself," Maggie said. She took a bite
of her toasted sandwich.

"Have you fallen for him?"

Maggie shook her head, looking around to see if anyone else
was in earshot. She saw no one she recognized.

Eileen lifted an eyebrow.

"I haven't fallen for him!" she protested but conceded, "I
may be falling for him."

"Don't split hairs, my dear."

"Is it that obvious?" Maggie asked, feeling a little sick to her stomach.

"Only to me." Her aunt laughed.

Maggie shifted in her chair, dropped her hands in her lap, and stared at them. "Of all the men in the world, why did I have to fall for this one? I mean, really, what's wrong with me?"

"We don't choose who we fall in love with," Eileen said quietly.

"I suppose we don't, but if this is God's idea of a joke, I don't find it funny." Maggie looked up at her aunt. "You won't tell anyone, will you?"

Eileen looked affronted. "Of course not! Besides, who would I tell?"

"Just promise me you won't go playing matchmaker or anything like that," Maggie said.

"I wouldn't need to. I see the way he looks at you." Eileen laughed.

Maggie looked at her aunt in alarm. "What do you mean?"

"When Jake Ballard looks at you, it's as if you're the only person in the room."

Maggie waved off her aunt's comment. "He's only looking at me like that because I'm a thorn in his side!"

"I don't think so," her aunt said. "Why don't you try finding a compromise? A solution where you get to keep your home and he gets to keep his golf course."

"I don't think he'd agree. He's said he needs to purchase the adjoining properties for his development to go forward."

Eileen shrugged. "There's a first time for everything. Go out for lunch, someplace neutral. Impress upon him how much the house means to you. Why you can't sell it. Ask him for a compromise that would suit you both."

Her aunt had given her something worth thinking about. Maybe they could find a solution that would keep them both happy. A solution where she didn't end up hating him. Because deep down, she didn't want that.

——ℓℓ——

The day of the Ballygap 5k Fun Run had arrived. Although it was a dull day, the whitish-gray sky was bright. Maggie had hoped for some sun but was grateful that at least it wasn't raining. A dry day was a good day in Ireland. She had arrived at the parish hall two hours before the official start of the race, to get things up and running. One team of volunteers would handle the cyclists, as their route was longer. The other team managed the walkers and the runners. They were out early, marking the roads with arrows in fluorescent orange paint and putting up signs along the course indicating the direction they were to follow.

The course for the walkers and the runners ran a loop around the town of Ballygap. It started at the parish hall, headed out of town toward the sea and along the footpath near the cliffs, and then circled back through farmland until it reached town again. The cyclists had an expanded version of the course. Tom Duffy and Sam Rooney would drive the car behind the cyclists.

Olive and Aunt Eileen were already there, getting the volunteers organized. Lily was there with the baby tucked into his pram. Eimear had been in the hall earlier but was now out along the route. Maggie loved race day.

She turned around and bumped into Jake, who'd just arrived with Noah and Roisin in tow. "Oh! Excuse me," she said. She tried not to stare at him in his running gear: a neon green shirt and black shorts, but it was just about impossible given how much she liked what she saw. She tried to walk away, but Jake took hold of her arm, his hand warm against her bare skin.

"How are you, Maggie?" he asked, searching her face.

"I'm fine."

Neither spoke and the silence grew larger between them.

"I'd better . . . go . . . get in line or something. I'll talk to you later," he said, and without looking at her, he walked away.

She watched him go, thinking about all the things that could never be for them.

Later that day, all the runners, walkers, and cyclists returned to the parish hall for refreshments. The event had gone without a hitch, except for the downpour of rain that came out of nowhere right at the end. They stood around in the hall, shaking off the wet as the rain slammed against the roof and the windows.

Although Maggie was busy helping Eileen and Olive in the kitchen with the refreshments, she kept an eye out for Jake. On her last run to place sandwich trays out on the tables, she scanned the crowded hall for any sign of him but did not see him. She hoped he was all right.

Noah and Roisin appeared, getting in line to get something to eat. She greeted them.

"I'll be bringing over some seaweed pesto on Monday," Maggie said.

"Great, I'm looking forward to it," Noah said.

"I'll let my mother know," Roisin said.

As casually as possible, Maggie asked, "Is your father here, Noah?"

Noah and Roisin looked at each other and grinned.

Am I that obvious? Maggie wondered.

"He got soaked, so he went home," Noah explained.

"Oh," Maggie said, unable to hide her disappointment.

She spotted April and Nigel and excused herself to talk to them. April seemed to be smitten, subjecting Maggie to endless conversations at work having to do with Nigel this or Nigel that.

"Hello, April, Nigel," she said. Although April's non-stop talk about the bird watcher got to be a bit much at times, Maggie thought the two of them were a good fit, and she truly was happy for them.

"How's the bird watching going?" Maggie asked. "What is it again? A corncrake?"

"That's right," Nigel said.

"Nigel's a birder, Maggie, not a bird watcher," April said.

"What's the difference?" Maggie asked.

"A birder travels to see birds; a bird watcher notices birds along his travels." Nigel picked up a triangle-shaped sandwich off his plate and stuffed it into his mouth.

"Can you tell me a bit about the bird?" she asked.

Nigel held up a finger as he finished chewing and then swallowed. "The corncrake used to be a common bird in Ireland. They're summer birds, of the family of crakes and rails. But their populations have suffered a drastic decline and are now threatened with extinction."

"Oh, that's awful."

"Guess what, Maggie?" April said, beaming. Maggie frowned. She hoped April would not announce something like she and Nigel were engaged.

"What?"

"They've spotted the bird on the McDougal farm."

Maggie stared at her assistant. "What?"

"That's where the bird has been spotted."

Maggie's mind raced with possibilities. She turned to Nigel. "Would the presence of this bird on the McDougal farm be enough to stop production of the golf course?" She tried not to get excited. She didn't want to get her hopes up.

"Maybe," Nigel said.

Maggie frowned. "Why only maybe?"

"Because I've yet to spot it myself," Nigel said.

"Not for lack of trying," April said. "Nigel is out there every day with his camera."

"But if you managed to find the bird, could it halt development of the site?" she asked, hopeful. She'd look for the bird herself if she had to.

Nigel nodded. "Most likely. Even if the bird was spotted anywhere near it."

Maggie was excited at the prospect of the little bird saving her home. And she prayed Nigel would find it.

CHAPTER SIXTEEN

ON MONDAY MORNING, JAKE opted for a late start, deciding not to go into the office until noon so he could take Noah and Roisin out for breakfast. As they were returning from the Sweet Tooth, he saw Maggie cycling toward his house. This was a pleasant surprise. He wondered what she was coming to see him about.

"Look, there's Maggie," Roisin said. "I bet she's dropping off the seaweed pesto."

"I hope so, it's all I've been thinking about since she mentioned it," Noah said.

Jake hid his disappointment. In the scheme of things, he was behind a jar of seaweed. He wouldn't let it get him down.

Maggie waved to them, pulled into the driveway, and hopped off her bike. "I've got the pesto." She took three jars out of her basket and handed two to Roisin and one to Noah.

"Noah, I'm going to run this over to my mom. I'll be right back," Roisin said.

"I'll be inside," Noah said. He took the jar from Maggie. "Thanks, I've been looking forward to this."

Maggie took a sleeve of crackers from her basket and handed it to Noah. "I've even brought some crackers for you. Though you could put it on anything."

"That's so great! I know what I'm having for lunch," Noah said.

"Let me know how you like it," Maggie said.

"I tried those tea bags together," he said.

"And what did you think?" she asked.

"It's pretty close."

Jake interrupted. "What's this?"

"I was talking to Maggie the other day at the shop, and I told her I was trying to find a tea bag that was as close as possible to high-grade machine-type chai latte. She suggested mixing these two different kinds of tea and she was right." Noah turned to Maggie. "I'm going to get an electric whisk, and then it will be just about perfect."

"Does that mean we can stop buying expensive takeout lattes?" Jake ribbed him.

"Probably not." Noah laughed. "Thanks again, Maggie." He disappeared into the house.

"I'd better get going," Maggie said.

"Hey, how much do we owe you for the pesto and the crackers?"

"You don't owe me anything. The first jar is on the house."

"Thanks."

Maggie raised the kickstand on her bike but seemed to hesitate. Jake was just about to say something when a car went by, honked their horn, and someone yelled out the window, "Hi, Maggie! Hi, Jake!"

They both waved. Jake didn't recognize who it was.

"Can I talk to you for a minute?" Maggie asked.

"Sure," he said.

"Do you have time?" she asked.

"I have all the time in the world." Finally, Maggie wanted to talk. To him.

She stood there, hanging on to the handlebars of her bike, and he drank her in: the way the breeze lifted a strand of her hair and blew it across her face, the eyes that reminded him of sapphires, the translucent skin that appeared impossibly soft, and those legs. How he'd like to run his fingers along the shape of them, memorizing the feel of every curve.

"Why don't you park your bike, so you're more comfortable?"

Flustered, she blushed and said, "Oh, all right." She leaned the bike against the stone wall in front of his house. She folded her arms across her chest.

Was he that difficult to talk to? To approach? He hoped not. Especially where she was concerned.

"It's about my home and your golf course," she said.

Jake wondered if they'd ever be able to talk about anything else. There were so many more important things to discuss. He wanted to know everything about her: What was her favorite season, and why? Where did she see herself in ten years? Did she like traveling? The list went on and on. But the fact that she was talking to him at all was something. Baby steps, he told himself.

"I had an idea," she started.

He waited.

"About how I can keep my home and you can build your resort. About how we can both get what we want." Her face was bright, and she appeared so optimistic that he hated himself for being the one that was going to burst her bubble.

Maggie Moran had no idea what he wanted. He looked at her lightly freckled arms and wondered how it would feel if they were wrapped around him.

"I'm listening," he said. He remained doubtful but kept his expression neutral.

"There must be some business use for my home that could work in conjunction with the resort. I was thinking a spa? Or I could move the health food shop up there. I mean if worse comes to worse, I suppose I could always turn it into a restaurant, but I'm no cook." She laughed, her voice taking on a higher pitch.

She chattered on, her face bright, and as she listed one idea after another, her expression open and animated, Jake felt something shift inside himself. Her enthusiasm and the way her face lit up at the prospect of being able to save her home undid him.

"You've given me a lot to think about," he said when she'd exhausted her list of possibilities.

She nodded, smiling. He'd never seen her so relaxed. So optimistic. Hopeful. Jake Ballard wanted to be the man who could make all her dreams come true. She reached for her bike.

"Maggie, before you go . . ."

She looked up at him.

"Will you have dinner with me tomorrow night? We can discuss your ideas." He smiled. "And we can come up with a solution that's agreeable to both of us."

Maggie rewarded him with a smile, and he wanted to bask in the glow of it.

"I would love to, Jake," she said, and she waved goodbye and pedaled off.

As she cycled away, he realized there was no way he was going to be able to tear down her home and live with himself.

CHAPTER SEVENTEEN

O N TUESDAY MORNING, MAGGIE was in her office, trying to balance the books. She blamed her lack of focus on the fact that she was going to dinner with Jake later that evening. It was all she could think about. She was looking forward to it. She also had to admit to a little apprehension. It had been awhile since she'd been on a date.

She thought about her wardrobe, trying to decide what to wear and what jewelry to pair it with. She had just decided on what type of shoes to go with when April appeared in the doorway.

"Tom Duffy is here. He wants to talk to you."

"All right," Maggie said, standing up from her desk.

Tom stood at the front door, smiling, his paunch hanging over his belt. Maggie regarded him warily. His good mood could only mean one thing.

"Tom, how's things?" she greeted him.

"Things are great, Maggie. How are things here at Slainte Mhaith?" he asked.

Maggie nodded. "The shop is doing great, thanks."

Tom hesitated, shuffling his feet. "I wanted to let you know personally that the county council has approved Greystone's planning permission."

Maggie's shoulders sagged. "They have?"

"The decision just came in this morning," he said.

Maggie's stomach clenched, and she held her breath. "What happens now?" she asked.

"It goes to An Bord Pleanála. Anyone who wants to register an objection needs to do so within four weeks."

Maggie nodded. "I'll get on that right away." She'd done her homework. She knew exactly what needed to be done to lodge an objection.

Tom nodded and turned to go.

Maggie called out to him. "Thanks, Tom, for coming to tell me."

Tom smiled. "We may not agree on this development, but we've always been friendly."

Maggie nodded and smiled, even though a seed of dread had taken hold inside her.

April came up behind her. "Are you all right?"

"I am. Thanks. I expected this." Her worst fear was now a concrete reality.

"Will I make us a cup of tea?" April asked.

Maggie shook her head. "No thanks."

"All is not lost, Maggie. Nigel said that as soon as he sees the bird, he's going to lodge an objection because of the corncrake on the land," April said.

Maggie nodded. "I am, as well." But she couldn't pin all her hopes and dreams on a bird that the birder was having difficulty spotting.

"Maybe we could get a petition going or something? To preserve the land for the bird," April said.

"That would be a great idea."

"I'll organize that. We can put a sign-up sheet right here on the counter."

Maggie thought of the other sign-up on the counter, for the coalition to protest the development of the golf course. To date, there were only six names on it: hers, April's, her aunt's, her friends', and Olive's.

"Okay," Maggie said. Her mind raced. She was happy to hand off the initial organizing of a petition to April while she collected her thoughts. She'd double-check with Nigel to make sure he was going to lodge an objection. But regardless, she would move forward with lodging her own based on the fact that her house was three hundred years old.

When the door to the shop opened, both of them looked up. Jake.

"Um, I'll go into the back . . ." April said, not taking her eyes off Jake, "and start that thing we talked about."

"Thanks, April." Maggie smiled.

"I came over as soon as I heard," he said. He reached out and touched her arm. "How are you doing? I just wanted to make sure you're all right."

"I'm fine," she said. What surprised her was his concern. About her. He wasn't boastful or bragging about receiving planning permission. This touched her.

"I'm glad to hear that," Jake said. "I'm still interested in taking you to dinner tonight."

"Oh, I don't know about that," she said. She bit her lip, unsure.

"I promised you we would discuss how your home and my golf course could coexist."

She smiled at him. He was trying.

"And you know what?" he continued. "If—when we come to a solution, then maybe we can talk about things other than the golf course or your home."

Maggie laughed. "You're right. What time will you pick me up?"

It was Jake's turn to smile. "Six? I thought we could drive up to Galway."

Maggie nodded. He'd given some thought to where he'd take her. This felt like the only bright spot of the day.

CHAPTER EIGHTEEN

J AKE LEFT MAGGIE'S SHOP and took his time heading back to the office. He wandered through the town center, hands in his pockets, thinking. The planning permission should have left him feeling victorious, but it didn't. He was more excited about going to dinner with Maggie than he was about receiving approval for his golf course.

Olive Enright approached him and caught his attention with a wave of her hand. "Have you heard the news?" she asked, excited.

"About the planning permission?" Jake asked. Didn't she realize he'd be one of the first to know?

"No, not that. Everyone knows about that," she said. "This is better."

He didn't know what she was talking about.

"Nigel Hayes has seen and photographed the corncrake on the McDougal farm," Olive said, enunciating each word. She had a look of triumph on her face.

"I'm sorry, Olive, but I'm not following you."

"The bird. That fella, Nigel Hayes from the Irish Bird Watchers Society, has been looking all over the place for it. A corncrake." When Jake didn't say anything, Olive sighed in exasperation. "The bird that's on the endangered species list?"

"I didn't know that, but I'm up to speed now. Thanks." He paused. "And you said it's been spotted on the McDougal farm?"

The elderly woman nodded. "Corncrakes haven't been seen around here for years."

Jake immediately knew what this meant. This bird would, no doubt, threaten his development.

"No hard feelings I hope, Jake," Olive said.

Jake smiled at the elderly woman. "None whatsoever."

They parted ways. Jake mulled over this recent development. His victory certainly had been short-lived. There would be objections lodged to An Bord Pleanála on behalf of this bird. It would end up pitting Maggie against him once again. Only one side could win, and as far as he was concerned, when it came to Maggie, he didn't want there to be a winner and a loser. As he walked toward his office, he thought about what the appearance of a corncrake meant for him. This could end up being a protracted battle through the courts. Not that Jake shied away from such things as he relished a challenge, but he didn't want to drag Maggie through the courts. Wouldn't put her through that. Not over a development. Not over land.

For the rest of the afternoon, Jake thought about a lot of things and most of them centered around Maggie. He thought about his future and every aspect of it: his family business, his role as a father to Noah, what he wanted for the rest of his life. And it seemed to him that all roads led to Maggie.

By the time he went home, he knew what he had to do.

CHAPTER NINETEEN

M AGGIE ASKED APRIL TO close up the shop that evening, as she wanted to get home a bit earlier, take the dogs out, and get ready for her dinner with Jake. She ignored April's comments about eating with the enemy. Jake had said they'd work out a solution and she believed him. She trusted him. There was no reason not to.

Once the dogs were walked, she came home, put on some music, and lit some scented candles, choosing a calming lavender. Although there was nothing to be anxious about, she was nervous about being alone with Jake for the next few hours.

She would have to tell him about her plan to lodge an appeal; it was best to have everything out in the open. But it was also the other parts of the conversation that made her nervous. What would they talk about? Did they have anything in common? And then she wondered if it even mattered, because she already knew she liked him.

She'd chosen a violet paisley maxi dress, and she slipped it over her head, thinking she would pair it with her diaphanous lavender shawl. She dabbed some perfume on her wrists. From the bottom of her wardrobe, she pulled out a pair of sandals and slipped them on. As she rooted through her jewelry box, trying to decide which earrings she wanted, there was a knock on her door. The clock read about ten minutes before six.

Arrgh! He was early. She took a pair of amethyst stud earrings out of the box and fastened them in her ears as she ran out of the bedroom, practically tripping over the cat.

Maggie threw open the door to find Jake standing there, wearing a pair of khakis and a light blue, textured short-sleeved shirt. Behind him, the setting sun streamed around him, casting him in a golden glow. The ocean created the perfect backdrop with the waves crashing against the surf and the cries of the gulls. The moment took Maggie's breath away. Their eyes met, and something sparked in his expression when he looked at her. Desire, maybe? She hoped so.

"Wow, Maggie! You look stunning."

Pleased, Maggie felt the heat creep up her throat and fan out across her face. She pulled the door open wider, "Come in, Jake."

Jake looked around before crossing the threshold. "I'm early, I know."

Rufus barked his greeting and ran to meet him. Daisy stayed near the sofa, eyeing Jake, watching him from a safe distance. And who knew where the cat was.

"It's all right, I'm ready," Maggie said. Her purse was on the table. She dug through it, pulled out a lipstick, and applied some. "Okay, let's go."

She took her shawl from the back of one of the kitchen chairs and draped it over her arm. She picked up her purse and said to the dogs, "Behave yourselves."

Rufus looked at her like the idea was questionable, and Daisy arranged her face into the mournful look she wore every time Maggie left the house.

Behind her, Jake asked, "Do they listen?"

"Not really." Maggie laughed. For Jake's benefit, she made a point of locking up the cottage, and the two of them walked toward his rental car.

They agreed that on the ride to Galway, they would not talk about her house or his development, and it was a relief to be focusing on something other than the thought of losing her home. That worry had consumed her thoughts these past few weeks, and she was glad for the break. For the first time in ages, she was out with a man she liked, and she decided she was going to enjoy herself. She liked the way she felt when he looked at her. Feminine. She felt light and expansive.

It was going to be a great night; she could feel it.

CHAPTER TWENTY

J AKE DROVE UP THE coast until they found themselves between Spiddal and Salt Hill. On his initial trip to Ireland, when he was scouting a location for his golf course, he'd stumbled on a small restaurant there at the end of a pier that served world-class seafood.

He kept stealing glances at Maggie as they drove along the coast. She looked stunning. When he'd gotten his first glimpse of her in that dress, she'd taken his breath away.

The conversation flowed. He told her about his life in California, and she opened up and told him about her parents. It touched him that she trusted him to share what must have been a traumatic time in her life.

As they walked into the restaurant, Jake put his hand on the small of Maggie's back. She looked up at him and smiled. When she did that, he felt like he could conquer the world.

The server led them to a small table in a dimly lit corner and waited until they were seated before handing them their menus. The ease with which they'd chatted on the way up disappeared. They buried their heads in their menus. It was almost as if they were afraid to discuss the main issue in case it ruined their good time.

They ordered their appetizers and entrees, then waited as the server opened a bottle of wine.

"Let it breathe, please, for a moment," Jake instructed. "I'll pour it."

As soon as the server was out of earshot, Maggie said, "About the golf course . . ."

Jake put his hand up. "Maggie—"

"Jake, I would like to be up front and honest about something," Maggie said.

"Of course," he said, yielding. He poured the wine. But only half a glass for him as he was driving.

"I can't tell you how appreciative I am that you're at least open to finding a workable solution for both of us," she said. In the candlelight, her eyes appeared almost violet.

"Um, Maggie, about that—" Jake started.

"Wait, Jake, there's something I want to say."

Jake smiled to himself. There was something he wanted to say, too, but he could see he'd have to wait his turn. He was more than willing to let her talk; he liked the sound of her voice. Her hair hung in curls over her shoulders, and he wondered what it would feel like to run his fingers through it. He imagined holding her in his arms. His eyes came to rest on her lips, and he wondered if they were as soft as they looked.

"I want you to know that although you have received planning permission, I'm going to lodge an objection to An Bord Pleanála. I've got two arguments, the first being the fact that my home is so old, and the second being the presence of the bird on the property."

The corncrake. It was the talk of the town.

Jake went to say something, but the server interrupted them with their appetizers—crab cakes for Jake and the salmon mousse for Maggie. Jake waited until the server was gone before picking up the thread of the conversation.

"Maggie—"

"I hope you're not angry about that," Maggie added.

Jake laughed. "Maggie, I'm trying to say something."

She blushed and mumbled, "I'm sorry. I just want everything out in the open."

"I would expect you to lodge an objection, but it isn't necessary," he said.

Maggie's fork paused in midair, halfway to her mouth. "What? Why?"

"I'm withdrawing my application for planning permission."

"Why?" she repeated. Faint lines appeared on her forehead, and Jake had a sudden vision of a future Maggie: older, wiser, lined and still beautiful. He hoped to God he'd be around to see it.

He shrugged and looked away. "It just isn't going to work out." He felt self-conscious about the real reason. If he admitted it, it might cause her embarrassment.

Maggie lifted an eyebrow. "I don't believe that for one minute."

He remained silent, wrestling with what to say. He wished he'd given this conversation more thought.

Maggie's expression softened. "Jake, would you just be honest with me?"

A million things ran through his mind. She wouldn't understand how he felt. There was the distance geographically between them. She was still young, while he had a son getting ready to go off to college.

He looked at her sitting across the table from him, lovely and expectant, and decided he wanted nothing hidden between them.

"Maggie, I know how much your home means to you."

She tilted her head to one side and smiled.

Jake looked away, rubbing the back of his neck. He laughed nervously, trying to find the courage to say what he'd been planning to say. He looked at the silverware on the table, straightening it out.

"Jake . . ."

Jake looked up at Maggie and blew out a breath.

"I realized that your happiness is more important to me than building this golf course." He laughed nervously and added, "It's more important than a lot of things."

There, he'd said it.

Maggie's eyes widened, but she said nothing. She sighed, stood up, and put her napkin down on the table.

A sense of panic swept over him. He didn't know what he'd expected her response to be, but he hadn't expected her to get up and walk out. How would she get home? Was she that insulted? Maybe the age difference bothered her.

But Maggie didn't leave. She walked over to him, a smile on her face, her eyes wet with tears. Jake looked up at her. She surprised him by leaning over and placing her hands on either side of his face. He swallowed, hard.

"Thank you, Jake," she whispered, closing her eyes, leaning in closer, and laying her soft lips on his. It took him only a second to recover from his initial surprise and delight before he took hold of her upper arms and returned the kiss. Her lips were even softer than he'd imagined.

Maggie broke away, looked around the restaurant, and gave a gentle cough. "Now, let's enjoy our dinner."

ello

Jake couldn't remember the last time he'd felt as content as he did that evening. Dinner went by too fast. He almost didn't want to return to Ballygap. Nothing had surprised him more than when she had leaned over and kissed him. He'd replayed that scene in his mind many times since it had happened.

Maggie rolled down her window, allowing the cool night air into the car as they drove back to Ballygap. She pulled her shawl around her shoulders.

"Are you cold?" he asked.

"No, I like the night air." She smiled. "I'm happy." He reached over and squeezed her hand.

"That makes me happy," he said, keeping his eyes on the road.

Much to Jake's regret, their evening was coming to an end. Ballygap was quiet this late at night. Most shops were darkened, except the petrol station and a few of the takeaways.

"Jake, now that you're not building your golf course, I suppose there's no reason for you to stay until the end of the summer in Ballygap."

Jake thought he detected sadness in her voice. He could only hope.

"I wouldn't say there's no reason for me to stay," he replied, looking at her knowingly.

Maggie blushed.

"But seriously, workwise, there is no reason for me to remain in Ireland," he said, his voice trailing off. He felt this topic was a great segue into a possible relationship between them going forward. But before he could explore the subject further with her, he was distracted by a strange red glow on the horizon as they headed toward Maggie's cottage.

"What is that?" Maggie asked, frowning.

Jake was just about to say he didn't know, when Maggie's home came into view. One section of the thatched roof was engulfed in flames. Jake blinked and stepped on the gas, pulling up a safe distance from the house. Maggie was out of the car before he could put it in park. He pulled out his phone and called the emergency services.

"The dogs and the cat!" Maggie cried.

"Maggie, what's your Eircode?" he asked.

She told him and he relayed it to the dispatcher.

Jake ran after her. The flames spread along the roof. She fumbled with the keys, trying to get the door open, but her hands shook. On the other side of the door, Rufus barked wildly.

"Give them to me," Jake said. He took the keys from her hand. "Step back." He pushed her back to safety.

He got the door open, and Rufus bolted out with Twinkle in his mouth. As soon as he was outside, he dropped the cat. Twinkle disappeared into the darkness, but Rufus ran to Maggie, and she threw her arms around him, pulling him into a tight hug. The sirens of the fire brigade sounded in the distance.

"Daisy! Where's Daisy?" Maggie shouted.

She dashed toward the cottage, but Jake held her back. "No, no you don't. Too dangerous."

"I have to get my dog," she cried. She called out, "Daisy, come on!" She put a foot forward again and Jake shook his head. "No, Maggie. No."

She fought him, sobbing. Again, he shoved her to get her away from the fire. Maggie collapsed on the grass and wept, her head in her hands, sobs wracking her body. He'd apologize later. Without another thought, he bent his head, tucked his chin into his chest, and ran into the house.

Thick black smoke filled the air. Jake coughed and crouched low, scanning the area for the dog. The heat was intense. The sound of crackling and whooshing filled the house as flames shot up the walls. All he knew was that he wasn't leaving the house until he had that dog. He shouted for Daisy several times over the din.

Jake covered his mouth and nose with his arm and ran into the bedroom, his shirt drenched, and his hair soaked with sweat.

"Daisy!" he shouted. "Daisy, come on, girl!"

In the bedroom, flames traveled from the drapes to the ceiling, spreading along the length of it. Jake knew he didn't have much time. He looked around the room, coughing and sputtering, and had just turned to leave when he thought he heard a whimper. He dropped to his knees and lifted the bed skirt. There, in the far corner underneath the bed, huddled the Irish setter, whimpering and shaking.

"Come, girl," he said, lowering his voice so as not to scare her any further. The dog didn't move. Jake realized the poor animal was paralyzed with fear. A flaming segment of the ceiling fell and landed on the bed.

"Daisy!"

The dog still did not move.

Jake half crawled under the bed and reached out, grabbing hold of Daisy's collar. He dragged her out, picking her up before she could retreat, and ran out of the house with her. The dog whimpered and shook in his arms. As soon as he was outside, he handed the dog off to Maggie.

"Daisy!" Maggie cried, her voice full of relief.

The fire brigade had just pulled up, and firefighters jumped off the truck and began pulling down the hoses. People came running along the footpath from town.

Tom Duffy arrived wearing sweatpants, a T-shirt, and sneakers, his face crumpling when he laid eyes on Maggie's house. "Oh, Maggie."

Jake moved away from the building, head pounding, glad that Maggie's animals were safe. Glad that she was safe. His pristine shirt was covered in sweat and soot and clung to his chest. He bent over, hands on his thighs, and burst into a fit of coughing. He felt as if his eyes were going to pop out of their sockets.

"Jake!" Maggie called, running to him. "Are you all right?" she placed her hand on his back. He was still bent over, trying to get his breath. "Jake, Jake!" He stood up and faced her. Tears streaked her face. He knew from the expression in her eyes how he must look.

Maggie turned her head toward Tom, who was waving an ambulance in closer.

"Let me get some help!" She ran off to the EMTs jumping out of the ambulance. Rufus followed her but Daisy remained at Jake's side. Jake continued to cough, trying to catch his breath. He could see Maggie talking to an EMT, gesturing and pointing at him.

The EMT ran over to him, and Jake sat down on the ground. He couldn't stand anymore. As he did, one side of Maggie's house collapsed. He hung his head, unable to look. Maggie knelt down next to him, rubbing his back. The EMT put an oxygen mask on him and told him to breathe. Jake concentrated on taking deep breaths.

"Sir, I'd advise a trip to the A & E to get checked out," the EMT said. To Maggie, he said, "I've rung an emergency vet to come out and look at the dogs."

"Thank you," Maggie said.

Jake was shaking his head. "No."

"Jake, please!" Maggie cried. He looked up at her. She looked over at her home and then back at him. She was shaking. He reached out for her and squeezed her hand. She didn't let go.

Jake shook his head. "Noah," he said, his voice hoarse.

"I'll look after Noah. Please, Jake. Now that's enough," Maggie said.

Reluctantly, he agreed to go. As they helped him onto the gurney, Maggie stood at his side, holding his hand. Daisy whined nearby. Maggie looked broken. She was pale, her eyes were wild, and her shoulders sagged.

"I'll get Noah and we'll meet you at the hospital," Maggie said, leaning over him and kissing him on the forehead.

"Please tell him I'm okay," he said. He didn't want Noah to worry. "Maggie, here's the keys to my car, you can drive that." He pulled his keys out of his pocket and handed them to her.

Maggie's tearstained face was the last thing he saw before they loaded him into the back of the ambulance and closed the doors. He lay back on the gurney and closed his eyes.

What a horrendous end to a wonderful night.

CHAPTER TWENTY-ONE

THE AMBULANCE PULLED AWAY, and Maggie pivoted and stared at the ruins of her home. The fire appeared under control. She could not see any flames, but the fire brigade continued to pour water on it. Her bedroom was no longer, and the thatched roof had caved in.

Her neighbor Peg O'Malley approached her, carrying a blanket. She looked the way Maggie felt: stunned. Without a word, she wrapped the blanket around Maggie's shoulders.

The emergency veterinarian arrived and looked over Daisy and Rufus.

"Maggie!"

Maggie turned and saw Eimear running toward her. She bit her lip at the sight of her friend, trying to stem another flow of tears.

Eimear pulled her into a hug. "Thank God you're all right! I came as soon as I heard."

"How did you find out?" Maggie asked. Eimear lived on the other side of town.

"I had just walked into town to get a cheeseburger and chips, and someone came into the takeaway and said your house was on fire," Eimear explained. She stood with Maggie, watching the fire brigade douse the burning house with water.

"Do they know what started it?" she asked, frowning.

Maggie shook her head, but she had an idea. It was most likely the lavender-scented candle. She'd forgotten to blow it out when Jake arrived early to take her to dinner. She swallowed hard. That fact was hard to get down. Jake had just handed her her home on a platter, and she'd gone and burnt it down with her own carelessness.

The vet suggested to Maggie that both dogs should go to the veterinary hospital and be further checked out. Maggie hugged her dogs, her tears spilling onto their fur. She was so grateful they were alive. Maggie and Eimear helped to get the dogs into the back of the vet's truck.

After the vet left, Eimear asked, "What can I do?"

Maggie realized she couldn't stand around any longer.

"I've got to get to Noah, Jake's son. Jake's gone to the hospital. Can you follow me in my car? I'll drive Jake's car to his house."

"Absolutely. Where are your keys?" Eimear asked.

"They're in my purse in Jake's car."

Maggie retrieved her keys and handed them to Eimear. Before she drove off, Maggie took one last look at her home, or what it had been reduced to. She still couldn't quite believe it. But she had to get to Noah.

She drove Jake's car back to his house, numb. Eimear followed her.

The lights at Jake's house were all ablaze. As soon as she pulled in, Noah appeared in the doorway with Roisin by his side. Maggie parked Jake's car, got out, and locked it. Eimear parked Maggie's car on the street and walked up to the house.

"Maggie!" Noah called.

"I came over as soon as I could."

"I got a text from Dad, and he said he was on his way to the hospital," Noah said, his voice cracking.

Maggie reached out to him. He looked so young and vulnerable. "He's going to be all right. We can go over right now." She made quick introductions.

"Yeah, I'd like that. Roisin, I'll text you later, okay?"

Roisin nodded. "Of course, Noah. Text me anytime. Okay? I'll leave my phone on." She slid her arms around his waist and hugged him. He buried his face in her hair. It was a tender moment and it brought tears to Maggie's eyes. She and Eimear turned away to give them some privacy.

"Okay, Maggie, let's go," he said.

"What else can I do?" Eimear asked.

Maggie sighed. "Oh, my Aunt Eileen! Can you ring her for me? Tell her what's going on, where I'm going, and if it's all right with her, I'll need a place to stay."

"You can stay with me," Eimear said.

Maggie shook her head. "You've done enough for me tonight. Besides, I know my aunt, she won't rest until she sees me."

Eimear nodded. "I'll take care of it."

Maggie felt lucky to have a friend like Eimear. "Come on, we can drop you off home on our way to the hospital."

Eimear refused. "Nope, waste of time. I walked into town, and I'll walk out." She nodded toward Noah. "You'll want to get to the hospital straightaway."

Maggie threw her arms around her friend and thanked her.

Eimear pulled away and coughed. "Okay, I'll see you in the morning." And before Maggie could respond, Eimear was out of the driveway, pulling her cell phone out of her pocket and heading toward her own home.

On the ride over to the A & E, Noah asked, "How bad was your house fire?"

Maggie's voice shook when she replied, "There isn't much left."

"I'm so sorry."

Maggie only nodded, the pain in her chest and the gathering tears making it difficult to talk.

———ele———

Lying in his hospital room with its fluorescent lighting, industrial tile floor, and wall of monitors, Jake looked as awful as Maggie felt. A nasal cannula had replaced the oxygen mask. Maggie hesitated in the doorway as Noah ran to his father.

"Dad!"

Jake pulled his son into his embrace and hugged him hard. "I'm fine." He waved Maggie in.

Noah stepped aside and Maggie stood across from him on the other side of the gurney.

"How are you feeling?" Maggie asked. She reached over and laid her hand over his. He squeezed it reassuringly.

"I've had a chest X-ray and bloods, and hopefully I'll be able to go home soon."

"Don't be in any hurry, Dad. Do what the doctor tells you," Noah said.

"Okay, boss," Jake teased. He looked back at Maggie, his expression grave. "How are you?"

She shrugged, feeling as if the events of the night were piling up on her and threatening to crush her. Her voice cracked as she said, "I don't know yet."

Jake gave her a sympathetic nod.

Maggie and Noah collapsed into chairs, and the hours ticked by as they waited for a doctor to come and speak to them. Despite it being the middle of the night, no one slept. The traumatic events of the evening had left everyone hyperalert and vigilant.

Eventually, a doctor arrived and told them that everything looked fine, but they wanted to keep Jake overnight for observation. Jake protested, but Maggie and Noah hushed him.

Maggie offered for Noah to come and stay with her at Eileen's, but Roisin's parents had been in touch and had offered a place for Noah to stay until they released Jake from the hospital.

Noah kissed his father goodbye and said he'd see him in the morning. The boy wasn't as anxious as when Maggie had first picked him up. Seeing that Jake was all right had reassured him.

"I'll head home," Maggie said. Her bottom lip quivered as she remembered that she no longer had a home.

"Come here," Jake whispered.

"I'll start walking to the car, Maggie," Noah said, and he disappeared from the room.

Jake pulled Maggie into his arms. "Everything's going to be all right. I promise."

Maggie buried her head into his shoulder and her body shook. Jake rubbed her back.

"Jake, I'm so sorry," she cried.

Jake pulled away from the embrace to look at her. "For what?"

Maggie stood up, tears streaming down her cheeks. "I never thanked you for saving Daisy."

Jake broke into a smile. "Is that what you're worried about?" He shook his head in disbelief. He hugged her hard and whispered into her ear, "You're not alone in this."

—— *ele* ——

Maggie arrived at Eileen's in the middle of the night to find her aunt waiting up for her. She drank the cup of tea Eileen made for her, and she relayed the events of the evening to her aunt, who looked pale and horrified. The reality of it cascaded down on her and suddenly, Maggie felt exhausted. Her aunt removed the cup and set it in the sink. She led Maggie to a guest room where she'd laid out a spare nightgown and bathrobe for her. Before she closed the door, she said, "Wake me for anything, even if you just need to talk." But that wasn't necessary, for as soon as Maggie's head hit the pillow, she was out like a light.

She awoke to the sound of someone knocking on her bedroom door. She opened one eye and looked around, frowning at the unfamiliar room. Then it dawned on her that she was at her aunt's house and that her own home was gone. She pulled the blanket up over her head.

There was a second knock.

Sighing, she rolled onto her back, pulled the cover back down and called, "Yeah?"

Her aunt popped her head around the door. "The man from the fire brigade is here."

Maggie sat up and reached for the bathrobe to pull on over her nightgown. "I'll be right down."

"Good, I'll make you some breakfast."

Maggie wanted to tell her not to bother but didn't have the energy to protest. She picked up her phone off the nightstand and turned it on. Once powered up, her phone emitted a lengthy series of beeps alerting her to new messages and missed calls. Quickly, she scanned the list. There were missed calls and texts from Lily and Eimear, from April, Olive, Tom Duffy, Peg, and many more. She'd catch up on them all later. Her first trip was to the bathroom to freshen up.

She made her way downstairs and found a man in his fifties or sixties sitting at the kitchen table. He was dressed in business casual, drinking a cup of tea. He stood up when Maggie entered the room. Eileen stood at the stove, tending to the rashers, sausages, and eggs that sizzled in a cast-iron pan. It smelled good, but Maggie was uninterested in food.

The man gave her a nod of acknowledgment. "I'm Joe Kelly, the fire investigator," he said.

"Maggie Moran." She felt foolish standing there in her bathrobe, but a part of her didn't care. She was going to feel even more foolish when she told him that she most likely was the reason for the fire.

"I'll be investigating the cause of the fire and should have a report ready in a couple of weeks," he said.

"Um, I have an idea of what could have caused it," she said, and lowered her head. She was aware of her aunt's eyes on her. Before she could lose her nerve, she said, "There was a candle burning when I left the house. I know it was stupid. Especially since my cat has a habit of knocking things over." It was important that she own it. No matter how much pain and regret it caused her.

"Okay, well, that piece of information helps."

Maggie felt sick to her stomach. She had burnt down her own house. The house she'd been fighting to save.

"Do you need to sit down?" Joe Kelly asked. "You look a little pale."

"No, I'm fine," Maggie said with a dismissive wave of her hand.

"She needs to eat something," Eileen said from behind her.

"Can I have your contact information?" the fire inspector asked.

"Yes," Maggie said, rattling off her cell phone number.

He handed her his business card. "Ring me any time with any questions."

Maggie nodded, numb.

As he turned to leave, he asked her, "You had homeowners' insurance, didn't you?"

Maggie nodded. "I did."

"That's good, because it's an impressive site. You can re-build," he said.

Maggie only nodded. She hadn't been thinking that far ahead. She didn't know what she was doing for the rest of the day, much less the rest of her life.

Eileen walked the inspector to the door, thanked him, and returned to the kitchen. She placed a plate of fried eggs, sausage, black and white pudding, a rasher, and beans in front of Maggie.

"Eat. Eat something." She then carried over a small plate of buttered toast, setting that down as well, and pouring her niece a cup of tea.

"Maggie, you know you can stay here as long as you like," Eileen said.

"Thanks," Maggie said. But she knew she couldn't stay there forever. She'd have to find someplace to rent while she decided what to do.

"What's the plan for the day?" Eileen asked.

"I need to pick up the dogs, and I suppose I should go home and see the state it's in," Maggie said with a sigh. She tried a bite of toast. "Maybe I can salvage some belongings."

Her phone rang. April's name flashed across the screen. Maggie picked it up and said, "Hello, April."

"Maggie, hi. I just wanted to make sure you're all right."

"Aw, thanks. I'm okay," Maggie said.

"Look, I've opened up the shop. Don't bother coming in, I'll handle everything." April said.

Relief filled Maggie. "Thank you so much, April."

"Can I bring you anything?"

"No, thanks, if you just take care of the shop until I get back that would be helpful," Maggie said.

"Righty-o. Talk soon," she said, and she hung up.

"April will look after the shop," Maggie told Eileen.

Her aunt nodded. "Are you sure you're up for going to the house?"

"I've got to find Twinkle," Maggie said. She knew the cat could take care of himself, but she wanted to find him just to make sure he was all right.

Jake came to mind. She wondered how he was doing. As soon as she ate breakfast, she'd ring him. The dinner in Galway felt as if it had happened a long time ago. The fire had reduced a beautiful evening to a blur of a distant memory. Everything felt ruined.

Just as Maggie and her aunt were getting ready to leave, Eimear and Lily arrived, their arms laden down with bags, which they laid on the table. They greeted Eileen and turned their attention toward Maggie.

Always gruff, Eimear pulled Maggie into a quick hug and then let go. "How are you doing?"

Lily hugged her, whispering, "Poor you. I'm so sorry."

Tears threatened to spill but Maggie maintained her composure, even if her voice shook a bit.

"I'm okay," she said.

"Would you ladies like some breakfast?" Eileen asked, loading up the dishwasher.

"No, we're good," Eimear answered.

"How's the baby, Lily?" Eileen asked.

"He's fine."

Eimear opened the bags on the table. "Lily and I went shopping this morning. We've got you some basics as far as clothes and shoes to get you through the next couple of days until you can get your wardrobe sorted."

"Some of the shop owners in town donated an outfit. They felt so awful for you. And as they know you so well, I'd say you're going to like what they picked out for you," Lily explained.

"Yep, it's got 'Maggie' written all over it," Eimear said.

"That's wonderful," Eileen said.

"The only thing we couldn't agree on was underwear," Lily said, laughing.

Eimear responded with a scowl. "We didn't have a clue as to what you like for undergarments. We went with full cotton briefs."

When Lily giggled, Eimear speared her with a look and said, "What's so funny? They happen to be the type of underwear I prefer."

Despite her pain, Maggie couldn't help but smile. Not only was she grateful for such wonderful friends, but they were able to get her to smile during a dark time.

"Show her the best part," Eimear said to Lily with a nod toward a canvas bag.

Lily lifted two white bakery boxes with "The Sweet Tooth" written across the top. "We thought you could use some comfort food." She opened the lids on the boxes to reveal an assortment of baked goods. There were eclairs, cream puffs, Neapolitans, millionaire shortbreads, muffins, and scones.

Next to her, her aunt cooed, "Oh, lovely." Tears pooled in Maggie's eyes.

"None of that, now. Chin up," Eimear said, placing her hand on Maggie's back.

Maggie nodded quickly.

"If you need anything at all, let us know," Lily said.

"I will. I can't thank you enough."

~ell~

Eileen insisted on driving Maggie to her house. As they neared, Maggie drew in a sharp breath. She just couldn't make sense of the scene before her. In the bright sunlight, the blackened hulk of her home looked almost obscene. Thin tendrils of smoke rose from the ruins.

Maggie got out of the car and approached her cottage with her aunt. Or what was left of it. The sun shone brightly, and the sky was a rare, deep, cloudless blue. Even the ocean was calm today.

It was the first time Eileen had seen the extent of the wreckage, and she responded by covering her mouth with her hands and gasping.

The place Maggie had called home, her safe haven, had been reduced to a pile of smoldering rubble. The air was acrid. She'd lost everything: her clothes, her belongings, important documents. Everything she'd accumulated in her lifetime existed no more. Looking around, she could see that there was nothing that was salvageable. Despite this significant burden, she was grateful she still had her dogs, and hopefully, the cat would appear soon.

Maggie's eyes filled with tears, and she swiped them away with her hand. She looked around, not knowing where to begin. How did one rebuild one's life from nothing?

Eileen put her arm around Maggie's shoulder. "Come on, now, everything is going to be all right."

"I feel as if I let them down," Maggie said. She pulled a tissue from her purse and blew her nose. She wore a pair of capris and a peasant blouse that one of the shops had donated to her. Her friends were right: all the clothes they'd brought over were things Maggie liked.

"Who?" Eileen asked.

"Nana and Granddad."

"Nana and Granddad? Why?" Eileen asked. Confusion spread across her face.

Maggie appeared bereft. "Because they left me their most prized possession and look what happened! A home that's been in the Moran family for over three hundred years, and I'm the one that destroys it."

"It's not like it was intentional," her aunt pointed out.

"It was my own carelessness. It might as well have been intentional."

Eileen drew in a deep breath. "It sounds cliché, but nothing lasts forever."

Maggie scowled at her aunt. "You're right. It sounds cliché." Maggie bent her head and sobbed, no longer caring who saw it or if she made a spectacle of herself. She kept wiping away the tears with the tissue until it was no longer of any use.

"Nana and Granddad didn't always live here," her aunt said. She pulled her sunglasses from her bag and put them on. "It's not like they got married and moved right in."

"They didn't? I thought they reared their children here."

Eileen shook her head. "No, Nana was a newlywed with bright ideas. Big ideas. Ideas that didn't include moving into a two-bedroom cottage with her husband's parents."

Maggie was stunned. This was a family history she knew nothing about. Her grandparents had never mentioned living anywhere else. But then, she had never asked.

"After they married, they moved to London for work."

"London! Nana and Granddad lived in London?" Maggie tried to imagine Granddad with his suspenders and pipe standing in front of Buckingham Palace. And Nana! Maggie's grandmother grew all her own vegetables, raised chickens, and made her own bread. She knitted jumpers and blankets and darned Granddad's socks.

"Tell me more," she said, curious about her grandparents' other life across the Irish Sea.

"After they were married, they rented a little flat in London, and both worked in factories."

Maggie didn't know what to say to all of this. She was trying to fix an image of her beloved Nana and Granddad in bustling London. But the picture remained blurry and grainy.

"Why did they come back?" Maggie asked.

"They hadn't planned on coming back. Ever. Well, that's how the family history went. They were looking to buy a home as the family started coming."

"I thought they reared my father in this house."

"They did," Eileen said. "After I was born, they lost their jobs. It's just the way it was. They hung on for as long as they could. My grandmother eventually sent them money to come home. They returned to Ireland, and your father was born soon after. They moved in with my grandmother and never left."

Maggie processed all this. She looked around at the land, the sea, thinking it was the same view that her grandparents and the rest of her ancestors had looked at for over three hundred years. She may have lost her home, but she still had that.

"The cottage was never meant to be their forever home, but that's what it became," Eileen said.

Maggie thought of how they had looked after her, given her a home and security.

Her aunt's voice softened. "When you go through hard times, you think you can never move on. But you have to go on living. And you start small, by putting one foot in front of the other. There's no other way. Besides, Nana and Granddad left you so much more than this house."

Maggie frowned at her aunt, uncomprehending.

"I remember that scared rabbit of a girl who arrived here at the tender age of fifteen," Eileen said, a faraway look on her face. "Nana and Granddad left you with other things. More important, intangible things."

Still frowning, Maggie asked, "Such as?"

"The person you are today, you are because of them."

Maggie stared at her aunt. Although she knew this to be true without a doubt, it was nice to hear someone else's take on it.

"Their unconditional love allowed you to become who you were meant to be: a free spirit, an independent thinker, a businesswoman."

Maggie had to agree with that assessment. Nana and Granddad's involvement in her upbringing after the death of her parents was stamped all over her life.

Eileen continued. "And because of that, you'll survive this tragedy and move on. Maybe not quite as you imagined, but remember, things don't have to be perfect to be good."

Despite her grief, Maggie had to admit that there was some truth to what her aunt said.

As they contemplated the blackened ruins against the backdrop of the bright blue sky and calm, sparkling ocean, Maggie thought she heard something and turned around.

Meow.

"Oh, Twinkle! Come here," she said, breathing out a long sigh of relief. She picked up the ginger cat and hugged him. Twinkle squirmed a bit, but Maggie petted him, and the cat responded by settling down and purring.

"We'd better get him home and give him something to eat," Eileen said. "Will I pick the dogs up from the vet?"

"That would be great," Maggie said. "Are you sure you don't mind?"

Eileen shook her head. "Not at all. Are they ready to be collected?"

"Let me ring them right now," Maggie said. She made the call and spoke to the receptionist, who reported the dogs were fine and ready for pickup. Maggie relayed this information to her aunt. Her phone rang again. This time it was Jake.

Maggie answered it and spoke briefly to him before hanging up.

She followed her aunt to her car. "Jake is home from the hospital."

"I'm happy to hear that," Eileen said.

"Do you mind taking the pets home by yourself? Jake is driving out to see the house."

"No problem, I'll put Twinkle in the front seat with me," Eileen said.

Maggie reached out and hugged her aunt, surprising her. Eileen, who was startled, laughed. "All right."

"Aunt Eileen, I can't thank you enough," Maggie said. "You've done so much for me."

Her aunt smiled and removed the cat from Maggie's arms. "It's what family does for one another." As she got into the car, she said, "Give Jake my best."

Maggie waited until her aunt pulled away. The sight of Eileen chatting away to Twinkle as they drove off brought a smile to her face.

She stayed at her home for a little while longer, deciding she would rebuild. Right here. And she would move on. And maybe someday her own children would look at the same view and walk the same ground their ancestors had trod upon.

CHAPTER TWENTY-TWO

J AKE WAS HOME FROM the hospital by early afternoon. He was still coughing, but he felt better, and the doctor had told him there was no longer a need for supplemental oxygen. She'd advised him to go home and rest and to take it easy for a few days. Roisin's father had offered to pick him up from the hospital, and Jake availed him of the offer, thanking him profusely.

His plan was to check in with Noah, then see Maggie. He hadn't slept well during the night at the hospital, as he was so worried about her. But his parents Skyped almost as soon as he arrived home, to make sure he was all right. Noah had called them and told them what had happened.

Their concern for him seemed to have aged them, and Jake, his voice still hoarse, spent a good five minutes reassuring them he was fine. Noah came and sat beside his father, joining the conversation, and Jake enjoyed the friendly banter that followed.

"Noah said you got planning permission for the golf course," his father said.

Jake shook his head. "No, Dad. Well, I did, but I withdrew the application. Greystone will not be building anything in Ballygap."

Don Ballard could not hide his shock. "What do you mean?"

"It will not work out here, that's all," Jake said. "I think we should look at Jamaica again."

Jake's mother interrupted. "Business doesn't need to be talked about today. When you're up to it, you can explain everything." She leveled her gaze at her husband and then said to Jake, "Whatever reasons you have for pulling out of the project, I'm sure they're valid."

Jake had done a lot of thinking while in the hospital, about Greystone and about his own future. There was a lot to discuss with his father when he returned home. But his mother was right; now was not the time to discuss business.

After they'd disconnected the call, Noah said, "I'm going to make dinner tonight."

"That's great."

"It'll be vegan though," Noah warned him.

"It sounds perfect," Jake said, picking up his wallet and his car keys.

"Hey, where do you think you're going? The doctor said you're supposed to take it easy and rest for a few days."

"I am. I'm going to see Maggie," Jake explained.

"All right. You get one hour and then you come home," Noah said.

Jake laughed, reached out, and ruffled his son's hair. "You're a great kid, Noah. Do you know that?"

Maggie was sitting on the grass in front of the ruins of her house when Jake arrived. She turned around when he pulled up and parked his car. He thought it looked worse in broad daylight. He took in the level of destruction. There was nothing that was salvageable. Not so much as a wall. Even the air around it smelled burnt.

When he got out, she walked over to him. The dark purple circles beneath her eyes alarmed him. She looked ghostly.

"Hi, Jake," Maggie said.

As she neared him, he could not resist. He pulled her into his arms and embraced her. She didn't cry, and she didn't push him away, either. When they finally pulled apart, they sat on the grass in front of the ruins.

"How are you doing?" he asked, his eyes searching her face. "How are the dogs? Have you found the cat?"

"I'm okay. The dogs are fine. And the cat made an appearance this morning and has gone home with my aunt. What about you?" she asked, concern weighing down her features.

"I'm fine," he reassured her. "Don't worry about me."

She nodded and looked back at the charred rubble. "I keep thinking if I look at the reality of it, I might get used to it."

Jake sighed. "Maggie, you need to give yourself time. It only happened last night."

He refrained from offering any other advice, suggestions, or solutions. Instead, he sat with her in her pain, neither of them saying a word. Jake was comfortable with that. The important thing was for her to know that he was nearby if she needed him.

The contrast between the blackened rubble of her home and the bright blue sky and the glittering ocean was both striking and disturbing.

"It's funny to think we just had a beautiful dinner together last night, and yet it feels like it was a thousand years ago," she said. There was a wistful expression on her face.

"Probably because so much has happened since then," he said with a sigh.

"Yes, so much has happened," she repeated, her voice breaking. She regained her composure. There was a hint of the old Maggie there behind those amazing blue eyes when she smiled and said, "You know, Jake, I had you all wrong. And for that, I am sorry. I'm glad I got to know you."

Uncomfortable with the praise but also pleased, the only thing Jake could get out was, "Thank you."

She leaned into him, and he put his arm around her.

───ℓℓ───

Noah had prepared an ambitious beetroot and squash Wellington, which he served with Maggie's seaweed pesto. Jake couldn't get enough of the seaweed pesto since he'd first tried it.

"We made this once at Roisin's house and I thought it was so good, I'd try to make it myself. It was a little tricky working with the puff pastry, but I managed it," Noah said.

Jake smiled at his son. "It's delicious. You should be proud of yourself."

Noah reddened and put a forkful of food into his mouth. "How's Maggie?"

Jake stared at his plate. "She's about as good as can be expected."

"Will she rebuild?"

Jake nodded. Maggie had told him she would, and he'd encouraged her. Before they parted ways, Jake told her he could help her with her insurance claim or source an architect for her. The firm he'd employed to draw the renderings of the golf course only did commercial work, but they might be able to recommend another firm for domestic dwellings. She'd nodded and said she'd appreciate any help.

"Um, look, Noah, I hate to tell you this but since Greystone won't be building the golf course, there's no reason for us to stay in Ireland anymore."

Noah laid down his fork and his mouth fell open. "What? We're not staying until the end of the summer?"

Jake shook his head. His son would never understand how much Jake didn't want to leave Ireland either.

"Oh, Dad, come on. I've got plans here for the rest of the summer." Jake was sure those plans included the girl next door.

"I know." He thought of his own plans he'd had for him and Maggie, which had disappeared overnight.

"Why can't we stay?" Noah pressed. He'd abandoned his dinner.

"Because I still have a resort to build this year and since it's not going to be built here in Ireland, I'm going to be scrambling to find a place for it."

"But we could have a real vacation, where we'd go sightseeing every day."

Jake hated to disappoint his son, but he did have a business to run. "Noah, there would be nothing I'd like more than to spend the summer with you exploring the rest of Ireland."

"Dad!"

Jake shared his son's frustration.

"When do we have to leave?" Noah asked.

"We should leave soon," Jake said. He was torn between being here for Maggie and his business obligations. "Within the next two weeks."

"Two weeks! That's hardly any time at all," Noah said.

"I am sorry," Jake said.

His son remained sullen for the remainder of the meal, and Jake decided to give him some space and not pressure him into conversation.

eee

Two days later, Noah stepped outside, and Jake locked the door behind them. There was some sun that offered a little warmth, and a slight breeze. Jake wondered if it ever got hot here. He was beginning to doubt it.

Jake clicked his key fob and the lights on his rental car flashed, signaling the car was unlocked.

"Come on, Dad, let's walk," Noah suggested. "It's not that far. Roisin will meet us up there with her parents."

Jake agreed and looked up at the sky, deciding it might not rain. He'd found that the weather here was deceiving. Twice he'd been caught in a shower while the sun was shining.

They were heading to the parish center, where the townspeople of Ballygap were having a surprise fundraiser for Maggie. As Olive had explained to him, they'd never be able to raise enough money for her to rebuild her home, but they'd be able to help her furnish it and start over. He'd bought a few booklets of tickets, and Olive couldn't hide her surprise. As he only needed two tickets for Noah and himself, he gave the rest away to townspeople he met during his day.

"Are you looking forward to heading back to California?" Jake asked. He'd talked to Nadine the previous evening, and she was eager to see her son.

Noah nodded. "I am, in a way. But I love Ireland."

Jake knew how he felt, and he couldn't help but wonder if it had anything to do with Roisin.

"Will you write Roisin once you go home?" Jake asked.

"Come on, Dad, keep up. It's the twenty-first century. I will not be writing letters, but we've agreed to email and text."

Jake shook his head, deciding not to point out that email was an electronic form of letter writing. "She seems like a nice girl," he said, hoping to open a conversation and maybe get some information out of his son. But Noah remained silent.

Trying again, Jake said, "Has Roisin ever been to the US? Maybe she could come for a visit some time."

Noah looked at his father. "Do you think so? She's been to New York, but she's never been to California."

Jake shrugged. "I don't see why not. Maybe next summer. We can ask your mother."

They walked on.

"Do you think you'll tell Maggie how you feel about her before we leave?" Noah asked.

Jake looked at his son, startled. "What are you talking about?"

"Dad, don't. You get all goofy when she's around." Noah laughed.

"I do not!" Jake protested, irritated. There were a lot of words he'd associate with himself, but "goofy" wasn't one of them.

Noah was still laughing. "Oh man, you are so lame."

"I'm not lame," Jake said.

"Yeah, you are. I just can't decide whether you act this way around her and do nothing about it because you're rusty or because you're enthralled with her," Noah said, eyeing his father.

Jake would not admit that it a was a bit of the former and a lot of the latter. He sighed.

"You should tell her how you feel before you leave," Noah prompted. "She's so nice."

Jake was not about to take relationship advice from his teenage son. But he was buoyed by the fact that Maggie had already gotten his son's stamp of approval.

"We'll see," Jake said as the parish hall came into sight.

"What are you afraid of?"

That was a good question.

CHAPTER TWENTY-THREE

M AGGIE LAID A PILE of new clothes on the bed and began cutting off the tags with a pair of scissors. Outside her window, a fresh load of laundry hung on the line in the back garden, flapping, waving, and snapping in the breeze.

She didn't know what she would have done without Jake, her aunt, and her friends. Or April, for that matter, who'd been a big help with the shop. Despite finding the bird and really having no reason to remain in Ballygap, Nigel had stayed on. And Maggie guessed that was because of April. Originally from Galway, he worked and lived in Galway city in the IT sector. But he was now commuting back and forth for the foreseeable future. Maggie was happy for them.

"Can you come with me to the parish hall?" Eileen called up the stairs.

Maggie frowned. "Now?"

"Yes, please."

"Do you really need me to go with you?"

"Come with me, I need to look in on something," Eileen said, ignoring Maggie's question.

"At the parish hall?" Maggie muttered to herself. She sighed and called down, "Give me five minutes."

She moved through the room, looking for her new poncho and slipping on a pair of sandals, also brand new.

Eileen was waiting for her in the kitchen with her purse hanging off her arm and her sunglasses perched on the top of her head.

At that moment, Rufus came running through the kitchen being chased by Sparky, Eileen's Jack Russell terrier. Sparky nipped and snapped at Rufus's heels. Daisy hid under the kitchen table. It wouldn't be long, Maggie reminded herself. She really needed to find a place to stay, and then her aunt could have her house back. And some peace and quiet. She was indebted to her.

"Ready?" Eileen asked, heading out the door without waiting for Maggie's response.

"I guess I am," Maggie said to no one in particular.

She climbed into her aunt's car and buckled up.

"What's at the parish hall?" Maggie asked.

Her aunt shrugged, pulling out of her long driveway onto the main road and heading toward town center. "Just something I need to check out."

"And you need me because . . . ?" Maggie asked, her question trailing off.

Eileen looked over at her and smiled. "Just thought it might be nice to get out of the house and go for a drive."

"To the parish hall?" Maggie questioned. She frowned and looked at her aunt, wondering what she was up to.

But Eileen remained silent for the rest of the brief journey into town. When they arrived, they saw that the parking lot for the parish center was full. They were forced to find a spot on the street.

"What's going on here?" Maggie asked as they walked toward the hall.

"I have no idea," her aunt replied, but Maggie eyed her suspiciously.

In the outer vestibule, they could hear the din of a crowd behind the double doors. Eileen held the door open and grinned.

—ele—

Maggie stepped into the main room of the parish center. It was packed with people. As soon as she appeared, a murmuring hush rippled through the crowd. On the opposite wall hung a huge banner that read, "We love you, Maggie."

Maggie came to a halt and looked around. She recognized just about everyone from town, from Lily, Sam, and the baby to Eimear and her fiancé, Ben, to April and Nigel, to Olive, to Dan Gentilhomme and his receptionist, Mary. There were people there whose names she'd never learned but whom she passed while cycling around town or walking down on the beach. People she only waved to.

With her mouth hanging open, she looked at her aunt. "What's going on?"

Before Eileen could reply, people began to approach, starting with Lily and Eimear, who pulled their friend into a group hug. "Maggie," Lily said, "You've been looking after the health of all of us for a long time. It's time for us to look after you."

Maggie swallowed hard.

Olive wrapped her in a hug, smelling of something citrusy. Dumbfounded, Maggie hugged her back. "The lavender spray did the trick," Olive declared. "I'm sleeping like a baby. We're all here for you, Maggie."

April was next, arm in arm with Nigel. April was jumping up and down with excitement. "Maggie, we'll all help you get through this."

Maggie looked around at the crowd, stunned. She fought to keep her emotions in check, afraid to embarrass herself.

For the next half hour, people came up to her and recounted things she had done for them. She was speechless.

The last people were Jake and Noah. "Jake," she mouthed, her features softening at the sight of him.

Noah approached her first. He shuffled his feet and looked down at them. Behind him, his father gave him a gentle nudge. The teenaged boy looked at Maggie, his face going beet red.

"Maggie, I've only been here in Ballygap a short time, but I'll never think of this town without thinking of you."

"Oh, Noah," she said.

Noah stepped away, and that left Maggie facing Jake.

"It's a great turnout, Maggie," Jake said, looking around the parish hall. "It says a lot about how Ballygap feels about you, and the feeling appears to be unanimous."

That sentiment hit Maggie like a club. Even though he was an American, she couldn't help but wonder if he included himself in that reference to the people of Ballygap. She took a good look around at the crowds of people, the laughing, and the general din of conversation. There were tables of raffle items for a draw that was to be held at the end, and there was another long table set up with coffee, tea, sandwiches, bags of crisps, and all kinds of desserts. It seemed many people had gone to a lot of trouble just for her. A lump formed in her throat.

"Hey, are you all right?" Jake asked. He reached out and took hold of her hand, giving it a gentle, reassuring squeeze. He leaned in and kissed her forehead.

Maggie returned the squeeze and was glad when he didn't let go of her hand.

"It's overwhelming," she admitted when she was able to get her voice under control.

"I bet it is," Jake said, "but so deserved."

She looked at him, kind of impressed that he thought that. What he thought of her mattered. She knew what she thought of him. He had risked his life to save her dog. He'd given up his golf course without a fight, saving her the hassle of lodging an objection. That told her all she needed to know about Jake Ballard.

Four days after the benefit at the parish hall, Maggie walked with Jake along the cliffs. It had only been a week since the fire. During that time, they'd met with the insurance adjuster at the site and he'd gone through the process of a payout. Jake had offered to be there with her and she was glad she'd agreed, as he asked questions that hadn't crossed her mind. He'd even taught her tai chi class for her. She was glad he was there. He'd said to her repeatedly that he wanted to be there for her.

It was funny to her how the thought of losing her home to a golf course had almost pitted her against Jake and sabotaged any burgeoning relationship. And now that the golf course wasn't going to be built, there was no threat to their relationship. But she wondered—more than once—if the loss of her home was too much of a burden at the beginning of any relationship. She often thought of that night they went to dinner. For a brief sliver of time, she had been outrageously happy. She wondered if she'd ever feel that way again.

"There is something I need to talk to you about," Jake said.

Maggie glanced at him, frowning at his serious tone.

"Now that I'm not building my golf course here, I do need to build it somewhere," he started.

"Of course." Maggie's heart began to race.

"Noah and I will be leaving Ireland soon," he said.

"Oh," she said. The thought of him leaving made her want to cry. Since he'd gotten out of the hospital, she'd seen him every day. Seeing and being with him had been the highlight of her days. He'd taken her down to Limerick to do some clothes shopping. He'd arranged with her to meet an architect with the caveat that if she didn't like this one, he'd get her another. And the day before, they did nothing fire related. He drove her down to Kerry, suggesting it would be good for her to get away. They spent the day in Killarney and had dinner there. He'd been right. She'd almost felt normal again being away from Ballygap.

But there were moments when he reached for her hand and gave it a reassuring squeeze. As they walked around Killarney, browsing and shopping, he'd held her hand. She liked the way her hand felt in his: smaller, safe, and protected. But most of all, not alone.

"Please understand that I have to go back, but I want to stay," he said.

"You have to work, Jake, and I'll be fine," she said, trying to convince herself as well as him.

"Look, why don't you take our rental? I've still got a month left on the lease, and the owner won't be back until the spring. It would give you some time to think about what you want to do next."

"That's very kind of you, but you don't have to do that," she said politely.

"It's a shame for the house to go to waste when it's already paid for."

When she said nothing, he added. "Let me contact the owner for you."

"All right," she said. A new home wasn't going to be built overnight, and she knew she couldn't stay with her aunt forever. "It's a little tense at my aunt's house. Not between my aunt and me, but her dog doesn't like my dogs, and forget about the cat."

"I'll take care of it for you," Jake said. "And when we leave, it's all yours."

"When are you leaving?" she asked.

"Next week," he replied.

That soon?

"When I go back to California, I'd like to call you. Or text you. Or Skype," he said. He laughed and rubbed the back of his neck.

She couldn't help but smile. "I would really like that." There was a little chink of hope there that he wasn't totally disappearing from her life, and she was going to grab onto it with both hands and hold tight.

———— *ℓℓ* ————

Maggie returned to work; she couldn't put it off forever and for the most part, it proved to be a good distraction. In the beginning, on some really dark days, she clung to the fact that she still had Slainte Mhaith. She was grateful for it.

But the day that Jake was leaving wound up being a particularly tough day.

Maggie slammed the jars of kale pesto in frustration on the shelves, moving the new stock to the back and rotating the old stock to the front. She felt as if she might never stop crying.

"Is everything all right?" April asked, coming up behind her. Maggie could only give a half-hearted nod.

"I know you're upset, but everything is going to be okay," April said. "And I'll help. I'll do whatever I can." She sounded so eager. Maggie smiled at her assistant because she knew she meant well, but April wouldn't have a cure for a broken heart. Still, Maggie knew her intentions were sincere. And the younger woman had been a godsend, managing the shop. She'd really stepped up to the plate.

"I'm fine," she said, setting down a jar a little too hard. Maggie grabbed another jar from the box, but April intercepted it and gently removed it from her hand.

"I'll stock the shelves," she said. She placed the jar on the shelf, its label half hidden. Maggie ignored it, not caring. April wrapped her arm around Maggie, giving Maggie's upper arm a gentle squeeze.

"Now, come on, let's get a cup of tea and light a candle," April said, leading Maggie to her office.

April made Maggie sit down in the chair behind her desk. She dimmed the light, took out her phone, and turned on the Bluetooth speaker. Birdsong filled the room. April lowered the volume and said, "Now, just sit back and close your eyes, and I'll get you a cup of tea." Maggie slumped forward in her chair, putting her head in her hands. Now the tears came. She had no business sitting down. There was work to be done.

"I have a lot of work to do. I have to ring Mother Nature and reorder stock."

April shook her head. "I did that yesterday. It's done." The younger girl lit a candle that purported to have calming effects. Maggie hoped so.

Maggie looked at her. "I really should get started on the end-of-month receipts."

"That's sorted, too," April said. "Just relax. I'll get you some tea."

Maggie stared at April, her mouth open.

It wasn't long before April was back with a cup of tea in a floral china cup. On the saucer, she'd put two biscuits.

"Oh, Maggie, it's going to be all right," April said soothingly. "Everything works out for the best." April set the cup of tea down in front of Maggie.

Maggie nodded, unable to find her voice.

"Will I sit with you for a bit?" April asked.

Maggie shook her head. She appreciated all that April had done, but she wanted to be alone. "No, thank you, I just need some time."

"Don't worry, I'll take care of everything," April said, closing the door behind her

Maggie sat back in the chair and let out a long sigh of frustration. Her eyes filled, and she bit her lip.

"I will not cry. I will not cry," she whispered. She wasn't crying over her lost home. Or over the fact that she'd lost everything.

She was crying over Jake Ballard. The tears started again.

No matter what she said to him, no matter how spiky she got, he always remained kind. He made her laugh. His humor caught her off guard. And he seemed to like teasing her in a lighthearted manner. After every encounter, she found herself going over the conversation verbatim in her head and trying to squeeze every nuance out of it. She examined what he said, his inflection when he said it, and his expression, trying to mine any bit that might show that he liked her. But since the fire, he'd been there for her. She had a ton of support from her aunt and her friends, but with Jake it was different. He could have just gone back home immediately, begged off, saying he had things to do to wrap up his stay in Ireland. But he'd spent every day with her, helping her with various tasks in getting her house rebuilt and by just being there.

And there was kissing and hand-holding. Maggie had enjoyed every bit of it. Surely that meant something? But she sometimes wondered if she wasn't in the right frame of mind to define these things.

She blew out a deep breath. This was utter madness. There was no getting past the impossibility of it all; it could never work out. He lived six thousand miles away. Although he'd asked if he could ring and email her, she couldn't help but wonder if they would drift apart. If they were doomed.

April poked her head in the door.

"How are you?" she asked.

"I'm managing."

"Let me get you another cup of tea," April said. Before Maggie could protest, she swooped in, took the teacup, and disappeared. When she returned, she set the full cup down in front of Maggie.

Maggie looked up at the younger woman. "April, I can never thank you enough. I am so lucky to have you here in the shop with me. I don't know how I would manage without you."

April brushed off the compliment. "Friends take care of each other."

Maggie smiled. "Yes, friends take care of each other."

April lingered in the doorway. "Jake Ballard is leaving today," she said.

Maggie nodded.

April leaned against the doorframe and bit her fingernail. "You know what might make you feel better?"

"No, what?"

"Telling Jake how you feel about him before he leaves," April suggested.

Maggie opened her mouth but didn't know what to say to that.

"He's leaving, and one of you needs to voice your feelings," April said. "I think you would regret it if he left and didn't know how you felt about him. And you don't need to add regret to your grief."

When had her assistant become so wise? Maggie wondered.

They heard someone enter the shop out front. April leaned her head back to see who was there, then turned to Maggie, smiling wide. "The universe must have heard me, because Jake is here."

CHAPTER TWENTY-FOUR

W HEN MAGGIE EMERGED FROM her office, Jake was drumming his fingers on the countertop. He'd decided he'd walk over to the shop to say goodbye, which he was dreading. But in the back of his mind, an idea had started to form and it was beginning to take shape. It was a radical idea but sometimes things needed shaking up.

As he tossed and turned the previous night, he'd thought of staying in Ireland. Running his business from here. Immediately, he'd dismissed it, thinking it was impossible. But for every argument he had against it, he was able to come up with a solution.

Maggie was getting some of her color back. The shattered look she'd had since the fire had begun to lift. Returning to work and building a new home had given her focus and purpose.

"Olive stopped over this morning," Jake said, smiling at the recollection of it. "She wanted to wish me well."

"That was nice. Are you all set?" Maggie asked.

"We are. Noah is saying goodbye to Roisin as we speak," he said with a smile he didn't feel. He glanced at his watch. "We've got to head to the airport soon." He drummed his fingers on the counter again. He was so excited to share his idea with her, and yet he was trying to summon up the courage to speak about it.

"You'll be glad to get back to California," she said.

Jake shrugged. "I don't know."

They stood across from each other in the front of the shop, not saying anything. He shifted on his feet. He decided to go for it.

"Maggie, I have an idea and you might think it's crazy but the truth is, I don't want to leave."

"I don't want you to leave," she said.

"That's good." He paused, gathering his thoughts. "That night we went to dinner in Galway, I had a lot of hope for us," Jake said. "I'd thought we might continue to see each other after that and see where things went."

"I thought that, too," Maggie said, her chin quivering. She looked down and fingered the hem of her sweater. "But then my house burned down."

"But then your house burned down," Jake repeated, feeling the weight of that sentence and how it had changed everything. How something so awful could obliterate so much possibility.

The sun shone through the shop window, illuminating them. Everything felt golden to Jake. And most of all, hopeful.

"The truth is, Maggie, I want to see you every day. I want to feel your hand in mine. I want to smell your perfume. I want to watch as the breeze lifts your beautiful hair from your shoulders. I want to take you in my arms and kiss you every day."

"But how would we make it work? You live halfway around the world, and I'm here," she said. Her expression was pained.

"I have an idea. I would like to come back to Ireland."

Her eyes widened as she took a step closer to him. "Come back to Ireland? When? What do you mean?"

He laughed. "I've been giving this a lot of thought. I travel all over the world, so my home base can be anywhere. It doesn't have to be in California."

Maggie blinked. "What are you saying, Jake?"

"I'm saying I'd like to move Greystone here. I'm going to have a discussion with my father when I get back to California. I have to leave today but I will come back. To you."

Maggie's mouth opened slightly and she said, "You'd do this? You'd do this for *me*?"

Jake laughed. "Maybe I'm crazy, Maggie, but I'm also crazy about you." It felt as if his heart had stopped. He added quickly, "But only if you want me to."

She exhaled a long breath. "Oh, how I want you to!"

Jake let out the breath he'd been holding.

He broke into a big grin, stepped toward her, and pulled her into a tight embrace. Her arms slid up under his and around his back. The feel of her was reassuring, and he went on hugging her. She held on just as tightly. Jake inhaled the scent of her and closed his eyes and smiled.

"I'm going to take Noah back to California. And then I will come back to you," he whispered into her ear.

Maggie pulled back, her eyes full of tears. "I will be here, waiting for you."

Jake nodded. "Good." He put his hands on either side of her face and kissed her, his heart feeling as if it were about to burst. He kissed her long and hard until she pulled away, breathless.

From the back of the store, they heard clapping as April said, "It's about time! Geez!"

EPILOGUE

J AKE NOW KNEW MAGGIE well enough after having been married to her for four years. And today, as they got ready to drive to the airport to pick up Noah, who was on break from college, he knew something was wrong.

Maggie looked pale and tired. The last few nights, she'd fallen asleep on the sofa right after dinner. He wondered if they were doing too much socializing. In the last two weeks, they'd been out three times. Once with Lily and Sam and Eimear and Ben, then to the christening of April and Nigel's baby boy, and then there was the going-away party at the parish hall for Peg, who had finally managed to sell her home and buy a condo in Spain. But more than that, Maggie was quiet. Unusually so. As he prepared the pot of porridge for the two of them, he kept his eye on her.

They'd rebuilt the house after the fire, a long bungalow with lofty ceilings and big windows with spectacular views. Jake had a memorial stone laid where the old cottage had stood that read: *Home of the Morans since AD 1711.*

Maggie'd just come in from the beach below with Rufus in tow. Funny, but since they'd married and moved in together, Daisy and Twinkle no longer went down to the beach in the mornings, choosing to remain behind with Jake. It hadn't gone unnoticed by him that the Irish setter followed him around the place. Whenever he left their home, Maggie reported that Daisy sat in front of the door, staring at it until he returned. Maggie found it amusing, and she'd laugh and say, "It seems I'm not the only one who has fallen in love with you." He brought the dog to work with him. The staff had fallen in love with her, but she generally remained in his office, napping on the floor close to his chair.

Jake whistled as he poured porridge from the pot into two bowls. He fixed Maggie's just as she liked it: a little honey, some raspberries and blueberries, and a splash of milk. Despite his concern over his wife, he was excited about seeing his son. Noah would spend the entire summer with them until he had to return to college in the fall. Jake had lined him up with a job in town, proud of the way Noah had matured.

Jake and Maggie sat down together at their kitchen table.

At the beginning, to pursue his relationship with Maggie, Jake had relocated Greystone Development to Ireland. Initially, his father had been reluctant to move the company but after a small stroke, he'd decided it was time to retire. When Jake mentioned the corporate tax rate in Ireland was twelve and a half percent, that had convinced his father. After providing a generous severance package to his employees in California, Jake rented commodious office space in the town center. His first hire was Delia, the widow with four children, as his assistant. He was able to continue doing what he'd always done: building golf courses and resorts around the world, with his home base located in Ireland. He had to travel a lot for his business, but when she was able, Maggie accompanied him.

"How was the beach?" he said.

Maggie looked up from her bowl as if she were just seeing him for the first time. He frowned at her pasty complexion.

"Maggie, what's going on?" he asked. A thought occurred to him. "Are you worried about Noah's visit?"

Her eyes widened. "Oh no, of course not. I'm looking forward to it."

"You haven't said a word, and you're very pale. Are you sick?"

"No," she said, "not in the literal sense."

"Come on, Maggie," he prompted. "We made a promise that there would be no secrets between us." Inside him, a small seed of worry sprouted, wondering if there was something bigger on their horizon that he needed to be anxious about. Maybe their age difference was finally bothering her. She was only in her mid-thirties, and he'd be fifty on his next birthday.

"I'm pregnant," she blurted out, her eyes wet.

"Pregnant?" he repeated, his mouth falling open.

"I don't know how it happened," she said, her eyes not leaving his face.

Jake couldn't help but grin. He knew very well how it had happened.

Maggie stood up from her chair so abruptly that it almost fell over. She righted it. Both Daisy and Rufus lifted their heads from their places on the floor. Maggie rushed around to Jake and sat in the chair next to him. Meanwhile, Jake tried to process what she was telling him.

She turned her chair to face him. "I know we only touched on the subject of children before we got married. And that you weren't sure you wanted any more because of your age . . ."

Jake remembered that discussion. Going into the marriage, he hadn't thought he wanted more children. His one child was close to finishing college and—he did some quick math in his head—this child would go off to college when Jake was almost seventy.

He looked at his wife. That gorgeous mane of dark hair, those blue eyes so full of hope and expectation. To have created a child with her—how could he not want that? A little spark of excitement went off inside him. Maggie had given him so much happiness, and this child was a result of that joy. He reached for her hands.

"That is the best news I've heard in a long time," he said with a smile.

Maggie's shoulders sagged and she exhaled loudly. "It is? Are you sure?"

Jake nodded. "You're going to be a great mother!"

He decided he was excited. This baby was going to be very welcome. He slipped into a daydream.

"Um, hello?" Maggie laughed. "I just lost you there for a moment."

"I was hoping the baby looks like you," he said.

She laughed. Jake leaned forward in his chair, full of joy, and placed his hands on either side of his wife's face. "I'm thrilled, Maggie. If you wanted ten children, I'd give them to you."

Maggie lifted an eyebrow and grinned. "Challenge accepted."

—— *ee* ——

Maggie gathered her purse and sunglasses and laid them on the kitchen table. She was waiting for Jake. It was time to head out to Shannon to pick up Noah, who was coming in on a flight from California. She couldn't wait to see him. Even though he was a child by a different mother, Maggie considered him her son, as well. She wondered how he'd react to the news of a brother or sister. Noah was a good kid. She knew he'd take it in his stride.

She looked around her home, her new family home, decorated in pale colors to reflect all the natural light coming in the expansive windows with their views of the ocean. On the mantle were three photos. An image of Jake and her on their wedding day sat next to one of the two of them with Noah at his high school graduation in California. The third photo was one Aunt Eileen had found in a box of photos and had framed for Maggie, a shot of her and her grandparents, taken when the three of them hadn't been looking. Granddad was leaning on a pitchfork, his arms folded across the top of the handle, grinning from ear to ear. Maggie was no older than twenty, her hair wild and blowing across her face, and she was laughing, probably at something Granddad had said. And Nana stood nearby in her wellies and her housedress covered with a big apron. But it was Nana's face that moved Maggie every time she looked at it. In the photo, Nana was looking at Maggie with an expression of pure love and wonder. If she looked at it for too long, she ended up choked up with emotion.

She pulled on a light sweater. There was a fierce wind blowing in off the Atlantic, and it was giving the June air a nip. Looking down, she rubbed her belly, thinking of the baby that was coming to them in January. She should never have doubted Jake. Without question, she knew he loved her. And they were happy. They'd created a loving home that would soon be filled with the presence of a child—or maybe someday, children.

Jake appeared from the bedroom, smiling. He wrapped an arm around her and pulled her close and hugged her. Pulling away, still smiling, he patted her belly and murmured, "So what do you think? A boy or a girl? Any feel for what it might be?"

Maggie laughed and shrugged, shaking her head. "Not a clue."

"I don't care, as long as it's healthy," he said. The excitement in his voice was contagious. She reached out tenderly to touch the side of his face. He took hold of her hand and kissed her palm.

"We'd better go," Jake said.

Maggie nodded and grabbed her things. As they walked out of the house together, she looked back, her gaze coming to rest on the framed watercolor of a corncrake that hung on the chimney breast above the fireplace. She couldn't help but smile.

———*ele*———

Stay up to date with news and releases and receive exclusive bonus material by signing up for my newsletter. You can find it at www.michelebrouder.com

ACKNOWLEDGMENTS

Many thanks to many people who helped with this book.

Niall Hatch from Bird Watch Ireland graciously helped me find the perfect bird for this story. He provided me with three possible birds to use to really put a thorn in the side of the Jake's development plans. I finally settled on the corncrake. Any mistakes in regards to this bird are solely mine and mine alone.

The County Council for their wealth of information they so graciously provided on planning permission and An Bord Pleanala in regards to building anything in Ireland. The process to obtain planning permission in Ireland is complex. Again, any errors are mine.

My fabulous beta readers, Rachel and Danette, who both have eagle eyes and make excellent suggestions.

For my ARC readers, the fantastic team who read the book prior to publication. Thanks for pointing out the typos, re-dundancies, and things that just don't make sense.

And of course, to you, dear reader, for sticking with me through this series.

ALSO BY MICHELE BROUDER

The Escape to Ireland Series
A Match Made in Ireland
Her Fake Irish Husband
Her Irish Inheritance
A Match for the Matchmaker
Home, Sweet Irish Home
An Irish Christmas

The Happy Holiday Series
A Whyte Christmas
This Christmas
A Wish for Christmas
One Kiss for Christmas
A Wedding for Christmas

The Hideaway Bay Series
Coming Home to Hideaway Bay
Meet Me at Sunrise
Moonlight and Promises

When We Were Young
One Last Thing Before I Go

Printed by BoD in Norderstedt, Germany